I0624423

Romance Sampler

The First Chapters

Renee Vincent

Renee Vincent
P.O. Box 114
Alexandria, KY 41001

ROMANCE SAMPLER: The First Chapters
Copyright © 2016, Renee Vincent
Digital ISBN: 978-1-944484-04-0
Trade Paperback ISBN: 978-1-944484-03-3

Cover Art Design by Renee Vincent
Stock Art by BigStock.com

Digital Release: November, 2016
Trade Paperback Release: November, 2016

Warning: All rights reserved. The unauthorized reproduction or distribution of this copyrighted work, in whole or part, in any form by any electronic, mechanical, or other means, is illegal and forbidden, without the written permission of the author.

This is a work of fiction. Characters, settings, names, and occurrences are a product of the author's imagination or are used fictitiously. Any resemblance to any actual person, living or dead, places, settings or occurrences is purely coincidental.

To all those who love coffee and books
as much as I do.

RENEE VINCENT BOOKS

Sunset Fire

Vikings of Honor Series, Book One

Chapter One

Connacht, Ireland AD 916

I shall marry this woman, Dægan Ræliksen decided. It had been over a fortnight since he first followed her through the green meadows to the waters of the River Shannon, watching her with intent. Observing her gave him great pleasure, and every day he anticipated her arrival, secretly longing to hold her in his arms. Only lately did he grow impatient with his desire for her, and this day, he settled on, would finally be the day he'd put his suffering to an end and make her his wife.

She stood amid the knee-high grasses and flowers in a white flowing tunic, hemmed with an embroidery of vibrant gold at the ankles and wrists. The sleeves were long and tapered. The bodice mildly followed the curves of her dainty torso, blooming into a tasteful neckline that allowed just a slight hint of cleavage to show before a single jeweled brooch fastened a matching cloak at her shoulders.

In days past, her tunics included colors of deep crimson, indigo, and sometimes an earthy beige. But today's choice was his favorite. She embodied the very likeness of a beautiful Valkyrie, save for her lack of weapons and fair hair. Her long russet curls were distinctly dark with shades of auburn glistening like radiant sunlight. Her skin was as smooth as fresh buttermilk, and her smile like a cool drink of water. She stood no taller than his shoulders, but she'd easily filled the empty space in his heart and the entire expanse of his mind for the past weeks.

By her attire, Dægan could only guess her to be an Irish maiden of wealthy descent. This too excited him, for in contrast to her apparent nature, she was rugged and spirited, riding her stallion as well as any of his mounted *hirdmen* to this specific place every day, yet still looking elegant upon it.

In the hours she spent alone, no man had ever summoned or demanded her presence. He found this quite odd, for she was old enough for bedding and young enough for bearing healthy sons. She came and went as she pleased, heedless to the fact that she was the object of another's longing. Instead, she'd often sing, tickling his heart with her exuberant voice and an Irish ballad that danced in his soul.

He was unexpectedly mesmerized by her, chained to the very thought that she could be his if he only dared to make his presence known. That in itself would prove to be the most difficult. He dreaded that his countrymen's reputation as savage foreigners would precede any valiant attempt at meeting civilly. He was a handsome man with a persuasive charm, or at least he was told so by other women who had fancied him. Yet he knew an effective *come-hither* approach would not be enough to sway the innocent soul before him.

He'd pondered his options last night over a scanty dinner of roasted rabbit and had come up with the idea of "saving her" from the rampant run of a conveniently spooked steed. It could be done easily enough, assuredly changing her views of a savage foreigner to that of a hero, and quite possibly obtaining the affable encounter for which he so wished.

But now, by midmorning, the idea seemed utterly ridiculous. There were too many opportunities for things to go wrong. The horse might not even spook to begin with.

Or if it did flee, he could have difficulties catching up with it. Or worse, the horse could rear and topple her from its back, gravely injuring her in the process.

Discouraged, Dægan continued to gaze through the trees and brush at his enchanting maiden, wanting desperately to step out and make himself known. Even though he could boast smooth-tonguing a few endearments in the beautiful lilting *Gaeilge*, he knew this woman only had to look at him to know he was not Irish. So how could he show his face without frightening her?

Every idea, no matter how promising it seemed, had its pitfall. He could only close his eyes and pretend to exist in a different world. And how grand a world he could envision behind closed lids; a place where they could meet without apprehension, smile without pause, and converse without falsehoods. What he wouldn't give to make that world a reality...

As Dægan opened his eyes in weary disappointment, he caught his breath to find her walking closer to him. His body became rigid, his heart raced, and only then did he notice just how fiery his blood could run through his veins. The distance between them diminished slowly with each of her steps, and he'd not a plan to remedy this turn of events.

Fleeting ideas swarmed his brain like dancing bees. *'Tis too soon in the day for pilfering and much too foolish to be thinking it.* The only halfway respectable idea that came to mind was to lie down and fake an injury. Perhaps he could say he'd fallen from his own horse, appearing helpless and in dire need of care. But for some reason, he did not drop to his back and put that plan into motion. He sat frozen, only staring as she stopped a few feet from him to peer blindly into the thicket.

"Who's there?"

Her voice was like springtime, genuinely sweet, with a pleasant, melodic tone that could warm a chilled soul after a long daily Erin rain. It was with this thought that he drew in a slow breath, catching her airy spiced scent that sifted between the summer-green leaves of the hedge plant separating them. He wondered if Valkyries smelled as good as she did.

Suddenly, from behind her, Dægan saw several dark figures emerging on the shores of the River Shannon. Although their distance was too far, he managed to make out that they were not alone. Coming closer were three more longboats flaunting red and white sails. He didn't recognize the men, but he knew from the shape and adornments on the prow that they were like him, Norse.

By this time, the first vessel had run aground and the men were descending from each side in large numbers. Sizeable fleets weren't usually merchants, but *hirdmen* who were following their chieftain into a devastating raid for booty or war.

Dægan reacted with lightning speed and pulled the Irish maiden to the ground before she could say another word. Without much effort, he stifled her screams of terror with a simple hardened hand to her mouth and pinned her to the ground as easily as battling a child. But a helpless child she was not.

She threw wide her mouth and bit his palm. When he retracted his hand, she launched her forehead into his nose, jarring him into a dazed state of mind. Everything around him went black and spun.

Despite that, he still felt her thrashing beneath him. He tightened his grasp as if his very will to stay coherent were cinched around her fragile little wrists. The only thing that kept him from passing out was his own agony, for it had now become his only thought. He forgot the woman, her sweet alluring voice, her carefree mornings, and her lighthearted dances amid the tall flowers of the Erin meadow. All he knew now was the pain in his face.

He heard her sudden intake of breath and assumed she finally saw what he'd seen—more men coming ashore. *You shall not die this day,* he wanted to say to her. *You shall not die.* But he hadn't the ability to reassure her or stop the flow of blood from his nostrils now soiling her dress.

Trying to be considerate, he wiped his upper lip on the

bear cloak that hung from his shoulders, although it was a prized possession, a trophy from the animal he'd killed in his bygone youth. He wouldn't have that bearskin at all had it not been for his father's words: *a man who slights caution presumes his death*. How foolish he was to dismiss those important words now just because his opponent was a woman and not a growling beast of muscle, claws, and teeth. However innocent her semblance was, his bloodstained fur was a painful reminder of his mistake. He vowed never to underestimate her again, starting with this unusually quiet moment. She was far too passive, and her sudden surrender seemed calculative.

Dægan spoke first. "I know you're frightened. But say not a word. Those men will hear you, and they will kill us both."

She looked at him as though he'd two heads.

"I'll not hurt you," he whispered again. He fixed his gaze on the deep pools of green in hers. And for a moment, time stood still. Even for her, he swore.

He noticed her trembling body and how tightly he held her wrists. He didn't mean to hurt her. It was not his intention to grab her and hold her down like some belligerent thug about to take his pleasures. It was solely to save her life, and if he hadn't forced her to the ground, they would have been seen, probably pursued, and undoubtedly slain.

With kinder eyes, he tried to give her comfort. "You must believe me. I'll not hurt you. I give you my word."

She seemed utterly confused by the viciousness of his actions and the contradiction of his noble words. He could only hope that his pledge meant something to her and that he didn't appear to be just an animal ready to ravage the reward of his successful hunt.

His heart went out to her, and he loosened his hold. But at that very moment, she brought her right elbow up to his nose again, hitting it with such force that it nearly blinded him.

She scrambled out from beneath him, and he could do

little about it. The pain was so excruciating, it threatened to split his skull in two. Never before had he taken such abuse from a woman that he actually contemplated the idea of her being a demon from *Hel*.

As blood poured between his fingers and down his wrists, Dægan tried to open his eyes. He saw his lovely hellion on horseback fleeing deeper into the woodlands and shrinking to a distant white blur. He grunted a swift harsh oath. Yet his greatest problem was not the damage done to his face, but the setback of her escape in plain sight. The once-quiet shores of the Shannon were now filled with shouts and commotion from the very men he so desperately tried to elude.

Somehow, Dægan sat up and crawled on all fours to his horse. He took extra care to stay low and out of sight, for it was better that the Northmen not know of his presence. Should she be captured, he'd at least have the element of surprise in his favor. With that in mind, he mounted the animal with dexterity and stealth, then booted his horse into a gallop.

His heart quickened, his body went numb, and his face cooled with the rushing wind. He felt nothing as he tore through the woods, dodging trees and ditches. His only thought was to catch up with her and keep her safe.

What seemed like a ride through eternity ended when Dægan saw the hindquarters of her horse and her white dress flapping like a flag in the wind. He looked over his shoulder to check the other men's advancement and realized they were still far behind as they had not yet come into view.

With the satisfaction of their distance, Dægan contemplated the difficulty of catching her without the others seeing *him*. He was greatly outnumbered, and his injury did not give him any advantage. One more hit to the face and he'd drop like a stone. Nevertheless, he expected the undertaking to be nothing short of arduous, and banished most, if not all, of the strategies that had come to mind, instead relying on the will of the gods.

He gained on her with every stride, and at first chance, he rounded her horse to the left to steal the reins from her hands. But his attempt failed, piloting him straight toward a labyrinth of trees. He barely steered clear of the oaks, teetering in his saddle to avoid crushing his knee, while shifting back to circumvent another. After surviving a few more low-hanging tree limbs, he emerged again, hot on her trail.

Upon seeing a stream in the approaching valley, Dægan drove his heels in and charged his steed forward in hopes of using the water to his advantage. He slipped his feet from the stirrups and pulled them up to squat on the saddle. As he steadied himself on his haunches, he prepared to leap when they crossed the stream so he'd have something other than the hard ground to catch their fall.

She saw him and her eyes widened with a paralyzing fear, failing to see the shallow muddy shore that lined the stream. Her horse fell swiftly to the ground and threw her over its head. She landed hard against the rocky embankment and lay there motionless in a crumpled heap.

Dægan immediately pulled back hard on the reins and cinched his horse's chin to its throat, making every attempt to avoid the same catastrophe. His horse stamped for traction and reared to relieve itself of the bit drawn in its mouth, only to dodge the oncoming path of her fugitive horse that was now running back across the water.

Dægan settled his horse and slid off, running into the flowing stream. He fought the push of rushing water around his knees, and once at her side, he rolled her over. A flash of bright red shocked him as blood had already soaked through her hair and into her eye socket.

Given the force of her fall and the seriousness of her injury, he half expected her to be dead, but was relieved when he laid his hand across her mouth and felt the warmth of her breath. What's more, her flighty horse had given a diversion that kept the other Northmen in the woods.

He looked her over one last time, determining that her

wounds were not life-threatening, and picked her up in his arms. He staggered slightly from the current and trudged toward his horse at the stream's edge. Mounting would not be easy, but then again, nothing he'd done this day was. He decided that being moderately careful with her wasn't necessary since she was unconscious, and tossing her over his shoulder was just as good and less troublesome.

Or so he thought.

Her dead weight made him teeter as he put his foot in the stirrup, and the blasted mud beneath him swallowed his other ankle deep in muck. Another harsh oath escaped him before he clutched the horse's mane and threw a heavy leg up over the saddle. As he settled in and lowered her body to his lap, he noticed the return of his own pain. It was a momentary awareness to which he paid little heed, for the woman was now in his possession, draped across his legs, her head cradled in his arms.

He touched her cheek, pleased with his reward—one she'd come to know soon enough.

* * * *

The sun started to set in the western sky above the loping green hills of Ireland. Dægan had been riding all afternoon, trying to reach Limerick before nightfall, where his fellow Northmen awaited him. But having an unconscious rider made it difficult for him to gain any ground. He decided, with dusk fast approaching, he should make camp for the night in the nearby forest, deep enough, though, to escape notice should the men who were after her come as far as he.

It was darker in the woods, and he regretted not finding a spot sooner. The trees stood quiet, absent the scurry of foraging nocturnal animals, and only the crickets were brave enough to proclaim their contentment with the night. Their collective serenade was just enough to convince him that he was being overly cautious.

He slid from his horse with the woman still in his arms

and found a perfect place to lay her down. The soft moss under a tall tree was his first generous offering of many more to come, for he was smitten with the Irish woman. Throughout his life as a merchant, he'd never before been fortunate enough to find such beauty without a high price. Some would argue that a broken nose was too high, but for him, it was a petty fee. He possessed the most valuable of all precious jewels in the world.

Having her was one thing. Having her never awaken again was another. It worried him that she was still unconscious. Even as he rustled around to beat the blackness of night—untying rolled hides from the saddle, tossing food and drink pouches about, and setting up camp—she never moved.

Her unresponsiveness was a quick thought, though, for the aching in his stomach kept the rest of his thoughts on a more primal level. Mostly of how his morning and afternoon meals were both missed, and that what he'd packed wasn't enough for his empty stomach, much less his new guest. A successful hunt and a good night's rest were what he longed for, but on this day, the gods seemed to prefer adversity to victory.

Fixed on turning the tables in his favor, he took some rope from his saddle and confined her to the tree. He hated the idea—detested it, moreover. But after one knot, he reminded himself of her lively spirit and wrapped two more lengths of rope for no other reason than common sense.

He also needed a fire. Not only to cook his meal but for ample warmth throughout the night. Be that as it may, he hesitated, for a fire would no doubt give their location away should the others still be searching for her. The idea that a fire was a necessary evil soon outweighed the risks, and before any more time was wasted, he started gathering wood and kindling for a modest blaze.

Within minutes, he set the kindling afire and proceeded to add wood as the flames reached for more. It was not hard to become entranced by the snapping and popping of the fire. It set the mood as he took in the beautiful sight of purity and grace that lay before him. *Chaste* was the word that contented him.

She had a shapely body, and a rip up the side of her dress bared one leg from mid-thigh to ankle. He envisioned the night she'd finally submit to his touch instead of fighting it so violently.

His own body stirred, and he stood up, trying to extinguish the sudden urges that swept through him like fire. He ached for a woman's touch and the heat of nakedness. They were pleasures he'd done without for many months. His journeys were few, and finding a woman of worth had become more important than his livelihood. And now that she lay only a few feet from him, it was a desire he couldn't just wish away.

As he took notice of the tent pitching beneath his kirtle, he left her alone under the night sky to hunt for a generous meal, lest she'd awaken to two shocking revelations.

* * * *

"M'lord, we couldn't find the girl," Einar said, spilling forth his best excuse. "We retrieved the horse she was riding, but she was not on it. I'd swear by the gods she has disappeared!"

Domaldr continued to stare out over the moonlit River Shannon, his growing irritation keeping him from turning around and facing his *hirdmen*. He was a freeman in the face of Norway's noblemen, but also a man who aspired to gain a noble's title, even if it was through sudden notoriety as opposed to the long road of accruing wealth and support from the local kinsman. Infamy was the shortcut to the title of *Jarl*, and the imminent war for Dubh-Linn was his surefire route to staking that claim—as long as he could survive long enough to get there.

"Believe me, Einar," Domaldr finally said, "women never just disappear. The willowy bitches will haunt you until the day you die. As will I, if you do not find her."

"But—"

"Our purpose here, as you're well aware, is to hold a hidden flank position for Sigtrygg Gale's western front. No one, including a feeble woman, was to know of our presence. And because of your incompetence, you've put me in a very difficult situation, as I'm forced to contemplate the worst with our little woman friend still at large. Surely you've seen that the dress she was wearing was not that of a slave but of a woman of importance. With that said, she's accustomed to others doing for her, therefore lacking the knowledge to take care of herself, much less know how to slip past six full-grown men!"

Einar's silence caused Domaldr to turn on his heels, taking first notice of the dark-haired Irishman among his other unspeaking warriors. "Who is this?"

Soren, a man not easily rattled, spoke for Einar. "We came upon him in the forest. He was hunkered down behind a fallen log, lurking—"

"I was hunting!" the Irishman corrected.

Soren shoved a quick elbow into the man's gut, doubling him over and forcing him to his knees.

Domaldr watched the man cough and retch, and rubbed his own temples fiercely, unwilling to deal with this much chaos so soon after their landing. He stepped forward, eyeing the young man at his feet. Even when the man was shrunk to his knees with his hands tied behind his back, Domaldr could tell he was exceptionally lithe and no stranger to hard work.

"Stand up," Domaldr demanded.

The man did as he was told, looking Domaldr in the eye, despite that he had to lift his chin a bit to do so.

"What is your name?"

"Breandán, son of Liam."

Detesting the pride in the Irishman's voice, Domaldr leaned in close to cut him down. "Sounds much important a name for just a hunter."

"If I knew *your* name, I wager I too could slight the importance of yours."

Domaldr raised the corner of his mouth in a bristly smile. "You've a sharp tongue, *Éireannach*. Much like myself. But 'tis not enough to spare you. From now on, you best speak as though your very life depends on it, Breandán."

Breandán's jaw clenched. "I swear to you, I was only hunting. I've no interest in the purpose of your gathering."

Domaldr ran his tongue across his teeth. "You don't look like a hunter."

"At first glance, you don't look like a horse's arse. But we are what we are."

Normally, Domaldr would have choked the life from any man who'd make such a remark, but instead, he crossed his arms over his chest. "I actually believe you, hunter, which means there's no reason for me to have you killed. Consider yourself fortunate. However, there's still the matter of *our* discovered presence, and setting you free would not alleviate that. As much as I believe you commonly speak your mind to the fullest of truths, I still don't trust you." Domaldr looked at Soren. "Secure him and guard him well."

"Aye, m'lord." Soren nodded, shoving Breandán forward.

"Einar," Domaldr said, putting a hand on his shoulder. "Let us talk."

Einar said nothing as Domaldr led him away from the group down to the banks of the Shannon. His uneasiness shone like a lantern in the night.

"I'm a patient man, do you not think?"

Einar swallowed hard. "Of course, m'lord."

"And you'd not dare test my patience, would you?"

Einar shook his head adamantly. "Nay. Never."

"Good. Then my burden seems to be lifted. When Sigtrygg asks who is to blame for thwarting his plan, I can say with certainty 'twas you."

Einar's breath caught in his throat. "If you must, m'lord…"

"Yet," Domaldr said, altering his approach, "your

idiocy will still be a chink in my armor. The slander of my good name would be a poor representation of my great ability to lead. I cannot have that, Einar. Surely, you understand."

Einar gazed at Domaldr, who feigned both sympathy and regret, yet all too suddenly, a hot pain ripped through his gut. Einar looked down and pressed his hands to the warm blood that saturated his kirtle and breeches. His legs grew weak, and he stumbled forward to grasp his chieftain, but Domaldr stepped aside, shoving him into the river. His body hit the water and floated amongst the red waves that rippled between the floating vessels.

Domaldr glanced up from his bloodied knife at the four men witnessing Einar's death. "Have Soren and two others go with you, and find that girl!"

Chapter Two

Dægan finished his meal of roasted meat and tossed the bones into the fire. Troubled with his inactive dinner guest, he sighed and wished she'd come to on her own. The excessive sleeping made him very nervous and the night far too long.

He rose from the fire, deciding that it was better to encourage her awakening than let any more hours of the night pass in a slow creep. Taking his knife, he cut a piece of hide sparingly and poured water from his skin pouch to soak it. He then knelt beside her, preparing to nurse her wounds.

As he dared to touch her, his eyes drank in the delicateness of her facial features, the fullness of her bottom lip, and the clean cut of her jaw that slipped into a graceful feminine neck. She looked so unlike the other women he'd known, and he found the differences to be quite refreshing.

He reached down and stroked a few locks of her hair that had fallen loosely across her chest, feeling the softness between his fingers. He was doubly pleased that its sweet scent was able to penetrate the swelling within his nostrils. He breathed in deeper this time and savored the fine oils she'd used, similar to the ones he'd sell in the marketplaces.

It took him back to his journeys in the Mediterranean, where silks and oils were plentiful, as well as the number of women who were eager to please the merchant strangers entering their ports. There were many to choose from, he recalled, all different shades of skin, with dark, enchanting eyes and sable, silken hair. Still, none equaled her.

Dægan wiped her brow with the soaked cloth, taking

care of the swollen red gash just below her hairline. He pressed the wet cloth to her abrasion and cleaned what blood had dried on her face. Often, he stopped to rinse the cloth, continuing his tedious yet gentle work upon her wounds as she slept.

Although she was unaware of his kindness, he thanked the gods for the opportunity to caress her, even if it was just for a short while. He knew, given the circumstances of their meeting, she'd not be as eager for his touch when she awakened. In fact, he was sure she'd fight twice as hard to escape him once she found herself alone in the dead of night with him. This time, he prepared himself for the worst. No more surprise maneuvers when it came to her.

Soon after he wrung the cloth out again, she began to stir. She moaned and showed signs of awareness, starting with the pain in her head.

"Shh…" Dægan whispered. "You're safe now. You're going to be all right."

Mara moaned again and opened her eyes, finding it hard to focus. She saw the figure of a man before her, calming her with his soothing voice. *Father… It must be Father. I made it home.*

She relaxed as she felt his hands caress her hair and heard his voice reassuring her that no one would hurt her again. It was definitely not her father, but probably a servant of recent hire. She closed her eyes, relishing the warm crackling fire and the strangely familiar scent around her.

She knew that scent.

It was a wonderful smell of masculinity and vigor, one she couldn't get away from. As much as she felt at ease, the strange aroma also surrounded her with a disturbing sense of danger. Trying to make out the figure before her, she blinked away the blurriness and squinted to join the double images into one. His face emerged from the haze, a sharply chiseled face with blond hair and kind eyes.

Blond hair?

Her breath caught, and once again she looked at the man she thought she'd escaped.

Where was she now? Where had he taken her?

Panic shot through her, and she quickly looked around, trying to recognize anything past the light of the fire. The darkness and the thick cover of the trees shading the moon overhead made for a difficult task. She was extremely nervous and dreadfully alone.

Frozen with fear, she watched him stand and walk to the other side of the fire. If he did so as a small act of kindness to make her feel more comfortable, it didn't slow her racing heart. His physical presence, no matter how far away he went, was still enough to terrify her. She couldn't take her eyes off him.

They gawked at each other from across the flames. She'd no idea what he was thinking or what he wanted from her. He simply folded his arms and smiled as if he found pleasure in knowing she'd realized he'd won the chase between them.

The man was a monument of beauty and power, sturdy as the ground beneath him. He had long blond hair, a well-groomed beard, and skin darkened from the sun. His hands showed scars and calluses from years of hard work, yet his clothes presented a different story, one of wealth and importance. His tunic was made of the finest wool, a lovely shade of cerulean with a tablet-woven braid around the neckline and hem. His legs were bare from mid-thigh down, and his lower calves were wrapped in the soft cowhide of his boots. His eyes revealed a sense of maturity and intelligence, yet even the darkness could not hide their color, for they were as blue as the ocean he sailed. Before her stood a being that only one word could suitably describe.

"*Lochlannach*," she breathed.

"*Lochlannach*, aye? I like the sound of that. It means *lake dweller*, does it not?"

She remained quiet.

"'Tis a good name," he said, sitting down. "Better than the ones I've been called before. You needn't fear me, this I swear. I know my word means naught to you. But I assure you, I won't harm you." He then took his dagger, still within its sheath, and tossed it to her.

She was surprised to find her hands tied together as the blade hit her lap, for she was far too engrossed with her captor to have realized it. The knife's hilt was intricately adorned with silver and gold, as was its sheath, and it was quite a substantial piece of weaponry for a barbarian to own.

No doubt stolen.

"Cut yourself free," he stated. "But I wouldn't run away if I were you. You're about a day's distance from home, and your knowledge of tracking landmarks will not help you under this night sky as the clouds are moving in quickly. Getting lost would be the least of your worries, for there are others who search for you. Although their determination may very well match my own, they're truly without care of moral conduct or your well-being. And as much trouble as I've gone through to keep you from these men, I cannot say for certain whether I'd have the might to do it again."

His words were a heavy warning roped with a little strand of humor, like the gentle twine that held her to the tree. She picked up the dagger and began to run the blade carefully across the rope, slowly shredding its binding until it gave way and fell into the folds of her gown. Aggravated, she threw the rope into the fire and watched it twist and ravel. As the rope diminished, so did her hopes for escape.

As a king's daughter, she was sure he'd use her to get what he wanted, and feared just how far he'd go. For that reason, she placed the dagger at her side slightly under her gown, just in case *his* moral conduct warranted drastic measures.

"We have traveled all day. You must be hungry." He pointed to the meat left on the spit. "Go ahead. I've already eaten."

She grabbed the skewer and devoured the meat quickly. She'd no idea how hungry she was until she tasted the roasted hare. It was still warm, and amazingly, the primitive meal was the best she'd ever eaten. Within minutes, the meat was gone, and she wiped her mouth of any residue, only slightly embarrassed to have eaten so voraciously.

"Thirsty?" he asked, reaching for his drinking pouch. He seemed to give thought to throwing it to her, but changed his mind. "May I bring it to you?"

His question spun in her head like a storm. As much as she wanted him to keep his distance, he asked for her consent instead of assuming it. She swallowed her fear and gave a nervous nod, for she was exceedingly parched.

He arose and approached slowly, keeping enough space between them as he sat beside her. He held the pouch in front of her. "Drink it all if you like. I've more."

She accepted it and drank just as quickly as she'd eaten.

"How is your head?"

Mara flinched at the approach of his hand, but he stopped short.

"Your head," he pointed out. "You fell from your horse. Do you remember?"

She touched her forehead and winced. "Where *is* my horse?"

"'Twould appear that it gave us a much-needed diversion to keep the men, who were after you, busy in the forest. I'm certain they've secured it back at the river by now. I would have. No sense in letting a perfectly good mount go astray."

"Then why did you?" she snapped.

His lips crept into a smile. "Because I took a beating in its stead."

She gave him a sideways glance. "I should warn you, a broken nose, reminiscent of the one you already have, hurts much worse the third time around."

"Ah, so I *do* have discolored eyes. I was wondering if you'd left any marks upon me."

She frowned. "You speak as though you enjoyed it."

He squeezed his nose gently between his thumb and fingers, which evidently brought a sudden pang between his eyes. "Hardly."

"Who were those men?"

"I know not," he stated with a shrug. "Their presence was as much a surprise to me as it was to you. But if you'd listened to me, they would never have known we were there in the first place, nor would you have that nasty bump on your head."

"So, this is my fault?"

His brows lifted. "I know the means by which I saved you from those men was not as noble as you'd have liked, but nonetheless, you've been saved."

"And I suppose you want compensation from my father worth my weight in silver, aye?"

"I want naught from him. Mayhap a bit of gratitude from *you* would suffice. Need I remind you, if not for my timely presence, you'd be a whore for those men on the River Shannon. Who knows how many would have had you by now. The way I see it, you're indebted to me for saving your life, not to mention your precious maidenhead."

She gasped at his arrogance but could only counter his rude boasts with a gaping mouth and a tied tongue.

He lifted his finger to her chin and closed her mouth for her. "My apologies, my lady. Perhaps we can start over. Say with introductions?"

Mara hardened to stone and crossed her arms. "I don't see how knowing your name will help matters."

"Very well. Then let us begin with yours."

She glared at him. He tilted his head to one side, and his eyes sparkled with benevolence as though he were truly interested in her and only her. His hair had fallen over his shoulder, and several small braids adorned with silver clips flashed in the firelight. They were minute, but incredibly detailed with interlacing designs.

Despite his unmistakably Norse features and what

she'd been taught to believe, he was well-groomed and clean. Quite frankly, he was the most beautiful thing she'd ever laid eyes on. He was not at all what she thought the *Fionnghaill* should look like, or act like for that matter, and she assumed that outlandish lies and exaggerated stories existed only because no one had dared to get close enough. By her own understanding, he was surely more than a savage…but no less than a man, who only inquired of her name.

Finally, she gave in, for names were harmless enough. "Mara. My name is Mara."

He smiled and boldly brushed back a lock of her hair. "Are you hurt anywhere else—Lady Mara?"

"Nay."

"Are you certain?" This time he peered closer. "You took quite a fall."

"I'm fine," Mara insisted. "It wasn't the first."

"Do you always make a habit of falling from your horse?"

Mara's mouth curled naturally into a smile, but she forced it away as quickly as it appeared.

"Ah, you find me funny," he pointed out.

"I find you odd and foreign. Nothing more."

"Perhaps I'd be less of those things if you knew my name."

Mara said nothing. Although she was remotely curious, she did not want to give him the satisfaction of thinking she cared. As she expected, he offered it all the same.

"I'm Dægan of Hladir, son of Rælik."

Mara liked the sound of his name, and it fit him well. But she refused to show any regard, acting as if his name were ordinary and, at best, a name that would soon slip from her mind.

But…his name clung to her thoughts, and she found herself almost brooding over it. Every idling recollection revolved around him: his voice as he spoke his own name, his exceptional generosity, his entrancing blue eyes, and what still seemed to be left unanswered—his reason for risking his life to save her.

Mara felt his hand upon hers, a sudden forwardness she hadn't anticipated. His skin was rather warm compared to the coolness of hers, and his adept fingers found their way around the sensitive underside of her wrist. He held her with a grip demonstrative of his tenacious might and control. But even as the little voice in her head told her to pull away and run, she couldn't. Her hand, he turned over, and in it, he placed the silver-and-gold dagger that once lay at her side.

"You can keep this with you tonight," he said, closing her fingers around it. "I promise you, I won't give you any reason to use it."

How could she doubt those words? Those eyes of dazzling blue? They were the inlet to his soul, where mystery and compassion were harbored, and no matter how hard she tried, she couldn't help but drown in them.

Dægan stood and retreated to the opposite side of the fire, standing massively before her like an old tree rooted in the ground. His arms and legs proved his masculinity and power, and the strength in his jaw accentuated his massive physique. His long golden mane complemented his features well, and his eyes could change like the tides in the sea, stern and intimidating at one glance, and gentle and honest at another.

While she was lost in her thoughts, he suddenly lay down upon the ground and covered himself with his thick bear cloak.

"You're going to sleep?" she asked.

"Aye," he said, shifting on the ground. "Even we *Lochlannaigh* must sleep, my dear."

"But I must get home! My father will be worried sick!"

"I'll get you home, I promise. But not tonight."

Mara's voice rose frantically. "When?"

"When I've an army of men to accompany me. 'Tis not safe for just you and me." He rolled to face her. "And you should put those thoughts of leaving whilst I sleep out of your mind. Even if you left right now, you wouldn't make it back before morn—that is if you didn't lose your way in the night. Let's be smart, Mara, and wait until my men can join us before we go traipsing back through hostile territory."

"I thought your kind always traveled in groups, roving bands of warriors, that sort of thing. Why do *you* not travel with your men?"

"Because for what I was doing, I didn't need their company."

"And what may I ask *were* you doing?"

He sighed. "If you must know, I had chosen a bride and was going to bring her home with me."

"A bride?"

"Aye."

Mara's temperament changed as she gathered the extent of his affections. "You seem quite fond of her."

"I am."

Mara kept watching him, liking the way he held the unknown woman in high regard. She softened a little. "Mayhap I should apologize. Had it not been for me and my untimely need of rescue, you'd likely be in her arms right now."

"Think naught of it," Dægan dismissed, repositioning himself beneath the cloak. "'Twill all work out soon enough."

"How did you acquire this woman to be your bride? An alliance?"

"Not exactly. I've *chosen* her, this is certain, but her father fails to know much about it."

Confused, Mara prodded deeper into his personal affairs. "And how do you plan to persuade this *uninformed* father of hers?"

"Well, I was hoping to offer him a dowry he could not refuse, along with an allotment of seven cows, but it might prove to be unnecessary considering my selfless, heroic measures this fine day."

Realization struck her soundly, and her words stumbled from her mouth. "You speak of me? And my father, Cathal? The King of Connacht?"

Dægan opened his eyes and leaned up on one elbow, stunned by her father's rank. He'd assumed her to be the offspring of some clan nobleman, but never had he given thought to her birth being that of the provincial leader himself. With her father being at the top of such a prominent hierarchy, it would surely be a more difficult situation for him to resolve. Yet, to the best of his ability, he pretended it was frivolous.

"If your father is indeed the King of Connacht, then it looks as if he's certainly the man with whom I must bargain."

Mara stood up, walked over, and kicked him square in his side. "How dare you!"

Dægan took the first strike, but caught her foot with the next attempt. He lifted her heel high enough that she lost her balance and fell to her backside. Still holding firmly to her ankle, he dragged her closer, avoiding her little fists that came like madness. He grabbed both her wrists and pulled them to his chest, forcing her to lean forward in his direction.

"How dare you!" she shouted again, fighting his grip. "You belittle my father with your conniving plan. He'll not fall for it any more than I have."

Dægan drew back in surprise. "You think this whole day has been naught but a conniving plan?"

"Aye, the men at the river, the chase, the rescue. 'Tis all a farce! I know your kind! You're all the same! Cunning thieves who pilfer from the weak and kill others out of greed!"

"I've never done such things!" he defended.

"Nay, you just look for women who will be naught more than your slaves soon after you take them to your marriage bed!"

Dægan's face flamed. "Is that what you think you are? A slave? Odin's blood, woman! I've been beaten, punched, and elbowed in the nose to the extent of bleeding profusely—and not for strategy's sake, my dear, but to truly keep you safe from the foreigners on the riverbank! I've gathered wood for a fire so you'd be warm. Hunted so you could eat. I've even given you a weapon to keep by your side to protect yourself, and all the while declaring to you my honest intentions of not—ever—hurting you!" He threw her hands back at her. "Now tell me again, who is the slave?"

Her sudden silence left him somewhat content that he'd gotten his point across.

He sighed and softened his expression. "I know you're afraid, especially being so far from home with a man preconceived as a savage. If that is all you think of me from this day forth, then so be it. But I'll not let you slander me as being a man without honor or without my kept word. I gave my word I'd take you back home, and I will. Furthermore, you're not my slave, nor do I have hopes of it later. I'm a chieftain who already has his fill of *thralls*, and I simply want a wife."

"You cannot be serious!"

Dægan snickered. "After what I went through today, I'd think there'd be no question."

Mara's breath drained from her lungs. "This cannot happen."

"Why not?" he asked, leaning in.

"My father simply won't allow it."

He took her into his arms. "Would *you* allow it?"

At first, Mara was shocked at how daring he chose to be by taking away the little comfort of space between them. She fought the effects of his sultry eyes, his rugged aroma, and his breath upon her cheek with all she had. But all in all, she could do little about it. She was torn between the spoonful of endearment he shoved down her throat, and the inviting warmth of his arms.

"You've not answered me, princess," he teased, drawing her closer to smell the oils upon her skin beneath her jaw.

"H-how *can* I answer you?" she shuddered as she felt the slight tickle of his beard.

"Just open your mouth and speak."

Before she could utter one word of resistance, he skimmed his lips over her chin and covered her mouth with a kiss. She couldn't move, for it was the first time she'd ever experienced one in all her nineteen years. The world around her ceased to exist as the heat and red-blooded strength of his arms molded her tightly to his chest.

She fell limp in his arms and welcomed the gentle caresses of his tongue parting her lips. He went deeper, tasting her, but was never rough or demanding. He only eased his tongue in as much as she'd allow. He played with her, pulled away, then delved back in, taking every sweetened gasp from her like a thief.

She couldn't help but respond to his every touch, and her virgin tongue dared to dance with his. He moaned softly in her mouth, a noise hardly to be heard, but it was enough to make her open her eyes and find his swirling in drunken lustfulness.

His unashamed forwardness would've sent her fleeing, but his embrace enveloped her with a passion she'd never felt before. A strange heat burned low in her stomach, and a rush of cool shivers trickled down her spine as his kiss fed both of those glorious feelings at once.

She froze, barely able to breathe as he dwelled near her lips. He was a mountain of strength and an endless vision of beauty, two things that both lured her and scared her to death. Caught in the very clutches of his hungry gaze, it was hard to discern what held her motionless. The pull of her own attraction to this man, or the dreadful fear of it?

Dægan drew backward. "You look frightened."

Chapter Three

What might have been a depraved reaction to a simple kiss soon became a pretentious rant of shame. Dægan put his finger to Mara's lips, silencing her. "Say no more. I don't want to hear that you made a mistake."

"But I did."

"You cannot tell me that you didn't want it. I felt it in your kiss, in your body as you fell against me." He reached up with both hands and cradled her face. "What you suffered was a desire that matched my own."

Again, she tried to defend herself, but with a flagrant lie. "What if I'm already betrothed to another man? A man who is far braver than you."

"Then I'd have to say, all bravery aside, he's not very attentive to you. He leaves you to fend for yourself in a cruel, dangerous world on a daily basis. But then again, why should he care what perils await you? He doesn't exist."

Mara harrumphed and substituted her perjury with simple honesty. "I cannot marry you. My father will not allow it."

"You've said that once already. But your father doesn't concern me. Besides, I've come to learn that most everyone has a price."

"You're foolish to think he'll care more for cattle and silver than his own daughter," she added.

"You're foolish for thinking that he won't."

"He'd never submit to such an arrangement, especially with you being a Northman. He'd more likely kill you."

"And this distresses you?"

"Aye," she returned quickly. "I don't want to see you die. If your death was my true intention, I would have already used the dagger."

"So, you trust me, then."

Mara hesitated. "*Should* I trust you?"

Dægan whispered his answer. "Aye."

"Should my father?"

"As well."

"But if you do not take me back to him as early as tomorrow, there will be no trust from which to build. He'll already deem you a thief, and no amount of heroism or grand marks of silver will be enough to exonerate you from your crimes. He'd take immense pleasure in hanging you."

Dægan measured her, but she remained undeterred, steady in her posture. Her bravery was astounding, and it convinced him that his choice of wife was a good one.

"Enough talk about your father. Let's forget about him for just one moment and get back to the way you accepted me. You resisted me much more at the river than you did just now. Why?"

"Because there's no use in fighting you. I know you're stronger."

Dægan shook his head and grinned. "Try again. Tell me why you let me touch you and kiss you so deeply. If that is not trust, I know not what is." He watched her posture melt and waited.

"I cannot explain to you why I allowed such inappropriateness. I assure you, 'tis not what I wanted."

"You didn't want me to kiss you? I could swear by the gods you wanted me the moment you opened your mouth to the caresses of my tongue."

Mara closed her eyes, trying her hardest to be angry at his insinuating comment, to be disgusted at the thought of his lips on hers. But she couldn't. His kiss was a sweet punishment, which taught her nothing except that his mouth was warm, compulsive, and truly pleasurable.

Entangled in her own confusing thoughts, she stood to leave. She tried to distance herself from the charismatic ogre, but he grabbed her wrist.

"You do realize that my hands are tied, Mara. If not for those men on the river, I'd have had you home by now and your father would be lifting his cup to me, whilst bequeathing your hand in marriage. You and I would not be arguing about this and 'twould already be done. Nevertheless, I'm expected home soon. And upon my return do my people expect a wedding. I'll not fail them."

"You'd marry me without my father's consent?"

"As long as I had yours, aye."

"And what makes you think you'll ever acquire my consent?"

Dægan sported a wry grin. "Anything is possible, my dear."

Mara ripped her hand away, crossing back over to the other side of the fire, not amused by his keen-witted absurdities. She sat there stewing over how much she hated being trapped by the night, dependent upon someone else's ability to get her home, *and* that he was confident anything was possible.

She heard him stir across the dying fire, but refused to look. While her thoughts ran red, he returned to her on bended knee and staked his dagger in the ground. Across his arm lay the thick bear cloak he'd been using to keep warm.

"What is this?" she asked coldly.

"The nights get cool under the shade of the trees."

"And the knife? Are you begging me to cut you?"

"Nay. I'm begging you to trust me."

Mara knew this gesture was more than just a crafty attempt to ease her mind. It was an endowment given to prove he cared about her, sensitive to the fact she'd be cold and miserable if he didn't give away half his bed. For the moment, she put her frustration aside and allowed her concern to come forward.

"What will keep you warm?"

"Worry not. I've two deer hides as well."

"But they're not as big as this cloak."

"Hm…I cannot understand how you can worry about me and kiss me as a wife would, yet you cannot conceive a marriage between us. Is it truly that hard to see?"

Mara refused to answer him.

"No matter," he replied. "I'll gain that consent, first by trust and then by love. Count on it, Lady Mara." He bowed his head and left to return to his makeshift bed.

Mara was speechless. In less than one day, she received a multitude of kindhearted acts from a man sworn to be her enemy. And why should he be an enemy? Because his height put him there? Or the fair hair that grows from his head made for a disreputable character?

Each unfounded reason was but a stone stacked high and wide to protect her, and she believed he'd somehow scale those walls of suspicion, mortared with doubt, to reach her heart on the other side.

Dægan spoke to her from across the fire. "Try to sleep, princess. We leave for Hlymrekr in the morning."

The place he referred to was strange to Mara's ears in pronunciation, but she assumed it was likely the recent Northman trading port of Limerick. She reluctantly lay down, curling beneath the cloak of bear fur. It was soft and warm and smelled just like him. Ironically, it calmed the restlessness of being somewhere lost between the near sweet rapture of Dægan's kiss and her father's far-off sheltering embrace.

* * * *

The light from daybreak had barely stretched above the horizon before dark, steely clouds covered the sky. Mara awoke first and sat up. The wind at her back thieved the morning sun's warmth, and the smell of moisture settled in the air. The fire between her and Dægan emitted a straggling line of smoke, and its ashes drifted on the breeze in hopes to escape the common fall of rain.

Before Mara could announce the approaching storm, she found Dægan already on his feet, saddling his horse.

After he gathered his things and fastened them down, he discarded the rocks around the fire and poured the last of the water from his pouch over the embers. They hissed and smoked, and when all was cool and wet, he used a fallen tree branch to dust the ground, removing any evidence of their presence. Moreover, he took some brush from the forest floor and scattered it over the pit, carefully covering every footprint and indentation on the ground so as to recreate the land as it once was. Not even a single bone from last night's meal could be found.

She stood, clutching the bear cloak around her shoulders, and moved out of his way as he took a look for himself.

"You're thorough, I see."

"Need I remind you of the scores of men who gave chase the moment they'd run aground? I'd be a stupid man to think they gave up their pursuit so easily." With reluctance in Dægan's eyes, he glanced at his bear cloak and held out his hand. "You'll thank me later when we are soaked to the skin, and 'tis the only thing kept dry."

Mara gave it up, and he rolled it around his forearm, cramming it into a pouch on the saddle. In one swift motion, he mounted and called her by name as if it were commonplace to summon her. She looked up, amazed by his handsome features. His golden hair blew in the wind, and his horse shifted and stamped. He was stunning, imperious as he sat upon the animal.

"Come, Mara. We must go." Dægan extended his arm as he rode around her, and she grabbed hold, leaping behind him on the horse. She pulled herself against him as they rode away, and soon they burst from the woods.

Mara saw the gleaming silver Shannon before her, a familiar sight that only taunted her with the knowledge she could very well have escaped her Norse captor and followed it north toward home. She watched it wind back into the hills as they headed in the opposite direction, fearing that, despite Dægan's promise, she'd never see home again.

Chapter Four

The thunder rolled like hundreds of heavy horses across a battlefield, shaking the ground as it passed above. The heavens opened and dumped its water in sheets without mercy. Within minutes, the bitter cold rain had seeped through their clothing and bled deep enough to chill the marrow in their bones.

To keep from shivering, Dægan directed his attention to the feel of Mara huddled against his back. She'd found a refuge beneath his wet hair, pressing as close to him as humanly possible. He couldn't ignore the warmth of her breath between his shoulder blades or the softness of her body. The thought of her naked stuck with him as readily as the thin wet tunic and shift clinging to her own body.

He cursed his crude musings. This was certainly not the time for indecency. If Mara only knew what had crossed his mind, she'd never trust him again. He willed depravity away and clutched her arms at his waist in silent reassurance. The shelter he promised was something he'd seen only once, near the river on his way to Connacht several days before. He hoped that his memory served him correctly—even prayed to the gods that it had, for the onslaught of needlelike rain in his face was wearing on his good sense.

Even his horse struggled to cope. The heavy downfall shrouded loose rocks upon the black slated ground beneath its hooves, and the animal slipped several times during their descent. It was a slope much steeper than Dægan had expected, but at least he didn't have to worry about Mara's ability to ride. She proved as competent in this jaunt as she had in yesterday's sprint. With that in mind, he lunged his horse off the incline and drove it faster to where he thought he'd seen the cavern.

Like a gift from Odin, it emerged from the thick gray fog. Although farther from the river than he'd remembered, the overhang was hospitable and tall enough even for his horse. Upon entering the shallow depths of the cave, Dægan relished the sudden end of the chastising rain. Tiny echoes of dripping water crooned an appeasing welcome as his horse's slick black body steamed.

"Are you all right?" Dægan's voice resonated within the cavern walls. Mara nodded as she shuddered, trying to absorb the warmth from his back.

"We must get you warm." He slid from his horse, landing on both feet, and reached for her. Without hesitation, she wrapped her arms around his neck, evidently too cold to care whose protective arms enveloped her. He smiled, for she'd morphed into a little child, burying her head against his neck, contrary to the fiery vixen from yesterday's affair. He cradled her close and savored the petal-soft lips upon his neck. If not for her shivering, he would've held her all day.

He shifted her weight to one arm and untied the hide from his saddle with the other. Giving it a good, hard shake, he covered her body and whispered, "Take off your wet clothes. I'll give you my cloak."

Mara reacted as if his words seared through her like a red-hot brand, and she clutched her arms in protest. "I most certainly will not."

"Then how do you expect to gain warmth in sodden clothing?"

"If you think I'll remove my clothes simply because you ordered it, you're sorely mistaken. I'll do no such thing." She jumped from his arms and kept the hide for herself.

"Listen, princess," Dægan said as he pulled off his boots and unbuckled his belt. "You, above all, should know this rain will hold us here for many hours, if not days. I'm not going to sit in wet, uncomfortable clothes when I've perfectly dry furs at my disposal. And I suggest you follow my lead."

Mara hadn't long to contemplate Dægan's candid advice before he'd completely disrobed. She gasped and turned her head.

He laughed. "You might as well get used to it, my lady. Soon you'll be seeing me this way every night."

"I will not," Mara argued over her shoulder.

"Will you close your eyes to me, even on our wedding night?"

"You're a stupid heathen of a man! How can you possibly think that I'll *want* to marry you?"

"I felt the tides turn last night—and so did you."

"Nonsense."

"Do you know what your problem is?" he asked, staring at the back of her head. "You don't trust *yourself*. You despise that you gave in to me so quickly, and for that, you question your own good sense. Your heart is talking to you, but you won't listen. You're denying yourself the chance to find love, a love that is different, foreign, and well beyond your dreams. I saw how you'd gaze upon the river waters in Connacht, farther than its shores, wishing for something greater. And now 'tis here in front of you, yet you fear the possibility of its wonder because 'tis not what your father wants. Tell me, Mara, what do *you* want?"

His poetic words coursed a path straight to her chest, almost knocking the wind from her. "You watched me?" The tone of her voice rose with shock and anger. If he wasn't standing behind her completely naked, she would've turned around and slapped his face. All she could do was repeat herself. "You *watched* me? For how long?"

"For many days," he admitted.

"Days?"

"Weeks, actually. I came upon your singing one morning, and 'twas the most beautiful sound I'd ever heard. Your voice was like the sweetness of honey on my tongue.

It lingered, and I couldn't rid its hold on me. I took pleasure in watching the simple life you lived and found myself wanting to offer you more. And each afternoon when you'd ride away, I was left with a feeling of utter sadness. I despised that feeling and decided I couldn't walk away from you any longer."

Mara gritted her teeth and tightened the hide at her shoulders. "No matter how charming a tale you tell, you're still a thief if you don't take me to my father!"

She heard him rustling behind her and prayed he'd grabbed the other hide from the saddle for himself.

"If I do that," he replied, "I'll put both our lives at risk. You know this. And by the gods, woman, turn around!"

Mara peeked over her shoulder, fully expecting to see him naked. But he stood with his hands on hips, his eyes tapered to slits, and his lower half covered with a reddish hide. It hung low at his waist, exposing his entire torso. His body was longer than she imagined, but just as well, for she'd never seen an unclothed man before. He was large and magnificent. His chest, his shoulders, his arms. Even the thin layer of dark blond curls running from his navel and beyond the obscurity of the animal skin was a beautiful sight.

"I'll take full responsibility for my theft if the time arises," Dægan said gruffly. "But until then, I'll keep you safe, first and foremost."

Mara tore her gaze from Dægan's body, realizing she'd been staring. She blinked and swallowed hard, trying to remember why he'd become so frustrated with her. Oh aye. She'd accused him of being a thief. At least he admitted doing so, which proved even beautiful men could be criminals.

On the other hand, she knew how the Irish didn't take kindly to lawlessness, especially when carried out by pagan intruders. She didn't want to see him punished for a misunderstanding and worried what her father might do to him.

"You must understand, Dægan, the longer we wait, the

harder 'twill be to explain all this. Let us return to my father before he judges you harshly."

Dægan looked her up and down. "Are you made of iron? Or is it your skull that bears the thickness? Not even I'd want to come face-to-face with those men on the river again. I trust they've come for bigger things, and even your faithful steed is not enough to satisfy them."

"We can go around them."

He laughed. "Ireland is only so big. It won't be long before there's an additional group of greedy Northmen making their advancement up another body of water. If you haven't yet heard, your Ireland is a prized piece of land. Your days of venturing to the Shannon alone are over."

"They're over because of men like you."

His brows lifted. "Better me than those on the four ships numbering in the hundreds, aye?"

Mara shrugged the frightening image from her mind and kept to the subject. "My father is not a man to keep to the Brehon Law when it pertains to the judgment of *Fionnghaill*. He'll not accept your atonement in the form of an honor price, nor will he hang you quickly. He'll more likely throw you in chains and cast you into an open pit where you'll die a slow death of starvation and exposure. Can't you see your death will be a heavy weight upon my shoulders? Why have you done this to yourself?"

"There's no sign of your father thus far. And I doubt this soon in his search, he'd look as distantly as Hlymrekr. By the time he does, I'll have rejoined my men and started our course for bringing you back home. Now, let's put this aside and get you warm. As much as you hate to admit it, you know you'll never get comfortable in those wet clothes you're wearing. Mayhap even catch your death of cold, which I'd rather keep from the list of things your father could hold against me. I can turn around if 'twould suit you."

Every moral bone in Mara's body told her this was wrong, but she was too miserably cold to care any longer. She'd have to discard morality, if just for a little while, and what would it hurt? Who would know?

"I promise," Dægan pledged, turning around to face the rain outside the cavern. "I'll not look."

"Are you giving your word?"

"If that is what it takes…"

Mara flipped the hide from her shoulders and lifted her gown up as quickly as she could. "All right, but if you so much as peek at me…"

"Hm…for the sake of curiosity, what *will* you do if I peek?" he taunted. "I always like to know what I'm up against. And the gods know I've underestimated your vigor in the past. Countless times, I might add."

She imagined Dægan had a big smile across his face. Since she'd never done anything like this before, she found herself constantly adjusting the fur hide around her body. Even with it, she still felt as nude as the day she was born.

Dægan tapped his foot. "Are you finished yet?"

She checked herself one last time. "I suppose so."

He whirled around and froze in his place. "I realize that 'tis not the finest of silk, but you look lovely."

Mara frowned. "You *are* a stupid heathen."

He neared her, pulling his rolled bear cloak from the saddle and wrapping it kindly around her shoulders. "Do you not think I know what beauty is? I've been on many voyages in search of iron, silver, gold, beaded jewels, silk, and the most desired scented oils. Many men have died to acquire these riches. I've even met fathers who've offered their daughters in exchange for such things. I've seen lands lush with green fields and wildflowers, mountains reaching higher than the air we breathe, and waterfalls cascading to the bluest of riverbeds below. And none of these come close to the beauty I see before me right now."

His words sank in swiftly. His description of her in a common animal hide was more than she could imagine any man ever saying. "I thank you for your kindness, although I'm still not sure what you're seeing."

"I see as a heathen sees," he reminded her.

"Hardly. If anything, you've proved yourself…"

"Worthy of you?"

"'Tis not what I meant to say," she insisted.

"But what you were thinking."

Mara hung her head. "What I meant to say is that you've proved yourself to be a man of great mystery."

"I suppose that is a compliment."

"Aye, 'tis. Most men I know can be as easily seen through as the streams that flow toward the rivers, and just as predictable."

"You've proven yourself to be just as mysterious."

He'd taken her words of subtle flattery and fed them back to her. "How so?"

"I never would've thought a woman would gain an upper hand in a struggle with me—twice you did that. Nor would I've guessed you to return a kiss."

Mara's face reddened. She'd tried many times to forget about it since it happened. Even as he spoke, it was difficult not to look at his lips and relive it.

"If memory serves me…I'd say you kissed me deeply."

"I was coerced," she defended.

"It didn't take much."

He grabbed the cloak from under her neck and pulled her closer. She shied from his intrusive eyes, the heat of his stare setting her ablaze.

"I know you're avoiding me because you feel 'tis right. 'Tis moral. 'Tis safer. But you needn't fear me."

Mara took a deep breath. "I do not fear you, Dægan. I simply do not know enough about you."

He drew back his face as if her choice of words stunned him. He released her and crossed his arms. "What would you like to know?"

Mara swallowed first before giving thought to his question. "Where do you make your home?"

Dægan's gaze deepened, and his posture softened. After a few moments' thought, he made himself comfortable on the ground and patted the place beside him.

Mara had always thought of herself as strong willed, impregnable in the face of temptation, but Dægan always seemed to find a way to push his way through with very little effort and carve his name on her rock-solid principles. Trust had now become a complicated virtue for her, a thin line between faith and fortitude. If she could help it, she'd not let him lure her across that line. Accordingly, she chose her own place to sit—away from him.

Dægan flashed his teeth in a grin. "Very well," he said, crossing his ankles. "Perhaps you've heard of my home. Inishmore?"

Unbeknownst to Mara, her jaw had dropped, and Dægan quickly made her aware of her reaction. "Baffling, isn't it? I suppose I've given you too much credit in thinking you didn't share the same feeble mind as the rest of your Erin neighbors."

Mara straightened at his blunt insult. "What is that supposed to mean?"

"It means you think your land is yours and no one else's. You think your Ireland cannot and will not be shared with others. But I assure you there're those, even with the noblest of Irish blood, who already share their lands equally with foreigners like me. Indeed, it may only be to keep peace, but nonetheless, they share. And why shouldn't they? 'Tis not as if we'd just landed here yesterday. My Northern forefathers have been here for more than a century. As any man wishes to find a more suitable place to call home, I too, am here, but—without the need to murder and steal, as you're so inclined to believe. So will many more after me. We are sooner your husbands and brothers than we are barbarous passersby."

"Indeed, you've landed here, but 'tis only a matter of time before your kind are rid from our shores. Even the mighty Romans were kept at bay."

Dægan laughed aloud. "The mighty Romans were only deterred because they feared the savagery of the Celts, and that savagery is what brought my forefathers here in the first place. But mind you, 'tis the rich land and the beautiful kings' daughters that keep the rest of us here."

"Does that include you?"

He raised his brow. "More or less, but it has never been enough to ground me. I'm still a seaman at heart, and if I could live upon a ship, I would."

The flutter in her stomach bit deep to the bone as she imagined sailing on an open sea. "Not I. I couldn't begin to fathom life upon a ship."

"What is it you fear? I know 'tis not water. I've seen you swim."

Mara saw the heat in his eyes with that statement and tried to hide her embarrassment in knowing he'd probably seen more than a woman treading water. "I suppose I'm like my mother in that respect. I've never known her to step foot off solid ground, or want to."

"What age were you when she died?"

Mara sat stunned by his question. "How did you know my mother had passed?"

"You've never spoken of her before, and usually a girl holds her mother in high regard. In my experience, women tend to follow their mothers' advice in most everything they do. You however, worry only about your father. Am I wrong?"

"Nay, you're not. I was only nine years old when my mother became ill and died. It seemed all too sudden at the time, but I came to learn that she suffered for months. My father sheltered me then, as he still does now."

Dægan fell quiet, as if to reflect on the sensitive subject, then said, "You spend your days by the Shannon because that is where you feel closest to her, aye? You go there alone because you want to be, and not because there's no one else to accompany you. And you sing the songs your mother taught you because you feel comforted by them."

Those memories and more danced around in Mara's head, harmonized by her mother's joyous laughter floating in sweet song. She was amazed at Dægan's careful yet poignant perception of things, and wondered how a pagan could have such an incredible outlook on life while taking notice of its tiny rewards.

"Now that I know your mother is no longer with you," he said kindly, "the days I spent watching you by the river feel quite intrusive. For that, I'm sorry." As the awful silence between them dragged on, Dægan spoke again. "Mara, I believe I've trampled on something I shouldn't have, and I'd be more than willing to speak of other things."

Mara was not so willing. "Do you still have your mother?"

Dægan took a deep breath. "I do. And I know she looks forward to meeting you."

"Your mother knows about me?"

"My mother is eager for grandchildren, and she's encouraged me to find a bride. She fears her age, but I swear she still has an iron fist and a stare that would send Thor running with his hammer between his legs."

Mara couldn't help but laugh with him, despite the reference to his pagan god. His laughter was delightful, and it was quite fascinating to learn so much about a man who'd been deemed heartless and murderous by everyone she knew. So much so that she decided to walk on the eggshells of religion. "Your god, Thor... He controls the storms in your world?"

Dægan's grin never left. "Aye, among other things. For the traveler, he's believed to protect, and for the warrior in battle, he instills bravery without fear."

"You believe in many gods. Is it not absurd to think there's a god for each detail of your life?"

"Is it not absurd to think one god can do it all?"

"Nay."

"Then your god is a very busy god."

"Do not mock Him."

"Ah, you misunderstand," Dægan said, raising his hands to cut short her incrimination. "I'm sure 'tis a belief passed to you by your mother, as was mine, and I'm well reminded to never forget what she has taught me, including when to politely change the subject."

"Being a man, I'd think you would learn most from

your father."

"Being a son, I've learned that mothers are oftentimes smarter than their hard-nosed partners and more aware of things around them. Where my mother is concerned, I'm not ashamed to admit that many of the skills I've learned are from her."

"Tell me one."

"All right." He lifted his chin in thought. "How about making you smile?"

"I'd hardly regard that as a skill."

"If I haven't the skill to make you smile, then it means you're truly enjoying yourself. Either way, I think the odds are in my favor."

"Possibly."

"Are you still cold?"

"Nay." Mara dismissed his question quickly, despite the goose bumps pimpling her skin.

Dægan leaned across the cavern floor and reached beneath the cloak, pulling out her leg. "You lie."

She jerked her leg back. "So what if I do?"

"Considering I aim to take you as a wife, I'd think you'd speak only truths to me. A husband doesn't take kindly to a wife's fibs, no matter how innocent they may be."

"Then you've more than proved my point. Men such as yourself always want things they cannot have."

"If you're going to group me with the likes of other Northmen, then you should remember we're quite able to take things we want. Hence, your Baile Átha Cliath, or as I call it, Dubh-Linn."

She stiffened, knowing he cared little for the port and more for the things he could acquire, like her affections.

He reached farther and slid his hand past her neck, into the mass of tangled hair that hung above her shoulders. He grasped a hold and brought her close enough that his lips were but a hair's breadth from hers. "You're correct in saying that desires often come from things we cannot easily gain—mine being that of your love. By all accounts, I do wish I could steal it. But I'm not that sort of man. I'll wait. Forever and a day...I'll wait."

Longing For Langston

Mavericks of Meeteetse, Book One

Brody & Liv

Chapter One

Brody Galven lifted his beer to his lips and sucked it down as he stared at the woman waiting tables at the other end of the bar. He leaned back in his chair and stretched his long legs. At the same time, he took a lengthy gander at hers. His goody-two-shoes older brother, Rod, would have scolded him for doing such a thing, but thankfully, he wasn't there. Instead, he chased his less than appropriate thoughts with the rest of his beer and continued to feast his eyes on her.

The locals knew her as Olivia, but he called her Liv. She had hair like midnight and eyes like ice, a combination that everyone in this backward town thought odd and unnatural. To Brody, they were what made her beautiful, as unique and unparalleled as a perky pink flower on a prickly cactus.

Though they'd grown up together, she never ceased to amaze him. No matter what the girl did, she could do it just as well or better than anyone.

She could fish.

Hunt.

Ride.

Sing.

And kiss like nobody he'd ever kissed before.

Brody smiled, remembering that first and only kiss

he'd shared with her.

It had happened one night on her twenty-third birthday. She'd been working the late shift at the Wagon Wheel and, as always, he sat in the parking lot on the tailgate of his truck waiting for her to get off work, so he could give her a lift home. When he heard the bar door burst open and his name squeal from her lips, he spun around just in time to catch her leaping into his arms. His cowboy hat hit the ground, and his heart soared. She'd finally landed an agent for her singing career, and before he could really understand what that meant, she planted a kiss on his lips.

At first, it was just a quick peck, an innocent gesture punctuating her excitement for something she'd tried for years to score. But as soon as she realized what she'd done, her smile faded.

Brody remembered how rigid Olivia's body felt against his as they held each other's gaze. The last thing he wanted was for her to push away and apologize. So, he bent and kissed her back. Only this time, it was slow and easy. Nothing felt more right than tasting her lips and feeling her body sink into his chest.

As he sat there, remembering how soft and warm her mouth felt on his, he also recalled the look in her eyes. He swore he saw a glimmer of unrestrained lust in them. As if at any moment, she'd tear his clothes off and have her way with him.

But what did he know?

A few seconds after he'd cupped her face and deepened the kiss, she pulled back and stared at him as if he had three heads.

To save face, he had played it off like no big deal and broke away from her with as much aloofness as he could fake. He swiped his hat from the ground and made some excuse about having to get her home right away so she could tell her mama the good news. Little did she know he was just trying to lessen the amount of time he had left to spend with her in case she was itching to discuss the matter exhaustively.

In hindsight, Brody was damn glad she hadn't called him out for crossing the line. He broke the friend code by following directions from something far more demanding than his brain. Most guys would've caught a slap across the face or a knee to the nether region for what he had pulled. Lucky for him, his Liv wasn't that kind of girl. *Just roll with it* was her usual motto.

Since then, Liv had never brought it up and he had never tried anything like that again. But it didn't mean his hormones quit raging. To the best of his ability, he resorted to admire her from afar and do his damnedest to keep it off the radar. Some days that was easier said than done—like tonight.

Though Liv had grown up a tomboy, Brody couldn't help but notice the feminine curves she crammed into her cutoff denim shorts. Hell, even the knot she tied in her shirt just below her breasts tempted him to pull it free.

Get a grip, Brody. She's off-limits and you know it.

He fidgeted in his seat, growing uncomfortable in his own tight denim jeans. Olivia Langston might be his best friend—heck, his only friend—but she drove him absolutely wild.

Brody adjusted his hat and leaned forward, resting both elbows on the table. He regarded the flirtatious smile she offered to a group of guys who'd ordered a round, and decided it didn't sit well with him.

She'd argue it was just for tips.

He'd argue it was too much.

That was the meat and potatoes of their relationship. If she wasn't doing something to either turn him on or tick him off, she was getting herself in a situation where he had to step in and save her.

From where he sat, he sized up all three of the newcomers, determining whether he'd need help if a fight broke out. Unfortunately, the folks in this establishment mostly resembled those from a retirement home rather than a cowboy bar. He'd be on his own this time.

Liv glanced his way as if she felt the weight of his gaze bearing down on her. To downplay the fact that he'd been caught staring, he picked up his empty beer bottle and shook it, signaling he needed another. She nodded once and dismissed him, only to offer another pretty smile to the three dudes in the booth.

Brody crossed his arms and growled under his breath. At times, he hated her job. Especially when she had to act all sweet and kind to a bunch of cheesy-smiling, smooth-talking city slickers who thought they were genuine cowboys because they wore a hat and boots. Brody took one glance at the shiny black leather gleaming from their Tony Lamas. They were no more acquainted with the dust and manure of a cattle ranch than he was acquainted with driving a Bentley.

A sudden surge of male laughter resounded from their corner, and Brody caught sight of a well-manicured hand reaching out and touching Liv's elbow. The man did his best to pour on the charm before his hand fell away and brushed her leg on the way down.

Brody tensed, ready to step in and crush every single one of those highfalutin fingers in his fist, but Liv would be furious with him. His chest burned as he tried to curb his temper for her sake. He bounced his leg on the ball of his foot, just itching to bolt out of his chair and teach this ill-bred urban cowboy a lesson in manners.

Liv stepped politely out of the man's reach and waited on the wannabe cowboy across from him. This guy seemed less forward than his friend, but no less fake. As he made some tasteless comment about Liv choosing the heat level on his wings, the third chump glanced up from his menu and spotted Brody glowering. He turned white and swallowed, elbowing his buddy. A few words passed between them before they all, including Liv, peered down the length of the barroom to where Brody sat.

He didn't have to stand to reveal his massive six-foot-three frame. He assumed he looked menacing enough as he stewed in his seat. His colorful sleeve of tatts on both forearms lent their share of intimidation as well.

Brody dared them to do anything—say anything—that was the least bit out of line. To his disappointment, all three shrank behind the wall of the booth and wrapped up their order with Liv.

She faked a smile in front of her customers and made some excuse that he was harmless, before she threw Brody a look and withdrew to the kitchen.

He didn't take kindly to the notion that she considered him harmless. When it came to her, he was about as harmless as a stalled stallion in a barn full of mares.

Minutes later, Liv rounded the bar with a bucket of beer and set it in the middle of the newcomers' table with another pleasant smile. She gave them some practiced spiel about her name should they need anything else before she patted one of them on the shoulder.

Brody rolled his eyes in time to see her marching his way. She stopped short of his table and slammed a beer in front of him. "Do you mind? I'm trying to work here, Galven."

Brody eyed the white foam racing to the top of the bottle, bubbling over the lip. He hated a beer full of head. "I'm going to need another one of these."

She lunged forward, planting both hands on the table. "I'm serious, Brody. Knock off the badass-boyfriend routine, will ya? I need their tips, and I'm not going to get anything with you giving them the evil eye."

Brody gazed into Olivia's gorgeous eyes. The temptation to look down her shirt killed him, but he never wavered. He had more respect for her than that, which was more than he could say for most of the customers who bellied up to this bar. Not to mention the trio of tenderfoots she had waited on.

"Are you listening to me?" she asked, stomping her foot.

Brody didn't mean to smile. It just happened.

Liv grumbled and snatched his frothy beer to exchange it. "I'm never going to get to Nashville at this rate."

Brody caught her hand, stopping her in her tracks. He liked the feel of it in his. To be truthful, he wished he could twirl her into his arms, tip her back, and kiss the daylights out of her.

She planted her free hand on her hip. "What now, Galven?"

The words she'd muttered echoed in his ears. *"I'm never going to get to Nashville at this rate."*

If anyone knew how badly she wanted to start her singing career in Nashville, it was Brody. For years, she'd dreamt of making it big and living off her voice instead of tips from yuppie city folk passing through on their vacation. After she landed that agent, everyone thought, including Brody, it was only a matter of time before she gained a big record deal.

That was last year, and still…she hadn't heard anything.

Brody softened his grip and patted the top of her wrist. "I'm sorry, Liv. I know how much that dream means to you." He peeled her fingers from the bottle and took a swig, enduring the watery taste of the flat beer. "I'll leave right after I finish this…skunk piss."

"Give me that," she said, smiling. "And you don't have to leave. It's fine."

He glanced around her at the three fellas in the distant booth. "You sure?"

"Yes, I'm sure. But chill out, okay? I can take care of myself."

"Yeah, well, I don't want anyone to take advantage of you. Men are pigs."

Liv's soft laughter immediately brightened his mood. "Are you including yourself in that statement?"

He thought about the many times he'd sweet-talked his way into a girl's heart. He could admit he was a giant pig with girls he didn't care about. But Liv was different. She deserved respect and a man who'd treat her right. Which was why he occasionally took out his sexual frustrations on girls who hadn't a care for their own self-respect.

"All men are pigs, Liv."

She blew out a dry laugh this time and shook her head. "I'll be back with your beer in a sec."

Brody watched her walk away, his gaze automatically falling to her tight little butt. He couldn't help but be mesmerized by its subtle sway, which had him wishing he and Liv weren't friends at all.

Yep. We men are pigs.

"Here you go," Liv said, handing him a fresh beer. He nearly jumped at the sound of her voice, unaware that he'd been carried off by his perverse sexual thoughts.

"Uh…thanks."

"You all right there, Galven?" She removed his Stetson and straightened his hair before plopping it back on his head. "Long day at the McKinley ranch?"

Brody cleared his throat, thankful she couldn't read his mind. He reached up and readjusted his hat the way he preferred it. Only Liv could get away with touching it. "Yeah, you could say that."

"Well, you sit back and enjoy your beer. I gotta sing in a few."

Liv dragged her fingertips along his arm and over his shoulder as she headed toward the stage in the back of the bar. He closed his eyes, relishing the feel of her touch for a few seconds while he tried to collect himself. As innocent as it might have been, that little brush of hers caused a whole cataclysm of sensations to run through his body. His groin tightened. His blood coursed through his veins. And his heart ached so deep in his chest, he thought it might burst.

He didn't know how much longer he could go through life just being her friend. He desired Liv more than anything, but it was too risky to tell her how he truly felt. Things would get awkward if he started sleeping with her. They always did when friends tried the benefits thing.

And what if she didn't feel the same in return? What if she didn't want to share that kind of intimacy with him? Or worse…maybe she *did*. And because she loved him so darn much, she'd turn down her chance to go to Nashville when the call came.

Brody's lids shot open the moment he heard the strum of her guitar and the sweet angelic tenor of her voice in the microphone behind him. Chills ran over his body every time she opened her beautiful mouth to sing.

Yeah…she'd be better off never knowing how he felt. She deserved to make it big and be happy. Besides, he knew one day she *would* get that call. And it'd be that much harder for him to say good-bye if he were sleeping with her.

Chapter Two

Taking a deep breath, Brody turned his chair around and faced the stage. He put on his happy face for Liv and drowned his aching heart with the rest of his cold beer. For the next few blessed minutes, he leaned back and enjoyed the acoustic one-woman show of Liv Langston, the only worthwhile entertainment offered at the Wagon Wheel—every hour on the hour.

He scanned the room as she hit and held a high note. About ten people, all of them regulars save for the corner booth of fancy Nancies, had gathered to mingle and be merry. Some came to eat. Some came to drink a few with friends. And some sat in quiet retrospection, smoking their choice of tobacco. But as of right now, every eye was glued to the dark-haired beauty in cutoffs. She rolled into the familiar bridge of an old Patsy Cline number, then segued into a classic George Jones song. He sat proud, watching her strum that beat-up six-string and listening to her rekindle new life into so many great vintage tunes.

As she brought her set to an end, a roar of cheers and applause erupted. Even a few piercing whistles split the joy and excitement of the meager crowd. Brody clapped as he watched Liv smile and bow in humble gratitude. It wouldn't be long before she'd be singing in front of thousands of fans. He just knew it.

Liv hung her guitar on the wall behind her and stepped off the platform to resume her waitress duties. Brody caught her attention and pointed to his empty bottle. *One more*, he mouthed.

She gave him the thumbs-up and walked between tables, checking on customers and snagging empties as she went. Just like that, the atmosphere of the Wagon Wheel returned to its usual state. The local drunkard, Bob Walsh, plopped his forehead on his arm and took another snooze on the slick lacquered wood of the bar. Mr. Corinth sat beside him, puffing on his cigar and watching Denver kick Cleveland into the dirt. His wife ignored the game and the few Bronco fans who sat adjacent to her. Instead, she perched on her stool, crocheting the beginnings of a tricolored afghan. On the opposite end near the restrooms, Professor Shoemaucker hid behind his newspaper as he always did on Monday evenings.

Everything was as it should be, save for the three guys in the corner booth. Brody kept refocusing his attention on them, waiting for one of the spoiled pretty boys to act out of line. He knew they would. He'd bet money on it. Especially the guy with the million-dollar smile and the thousand-dollar wristwatch. He had more flash than a vintage mid-century Kodak camera. Guys like that loved to be the center of attention and often went to extremes to acquire it.

"You're doing it again, Galven," Liv interrupted, handing Brody a full one.

"Doing what?"

"Sizing them up. Finding justification for kicking their asses." Liv seized his chin and drew his attention toward her. "Let it go. I mean it."

Though she stood no taller than five foot four, weighing in at a buck ten, Brody adored her confidence. She embodied self-assurance in the way she turned and sashayed down the aisle of empty tables. He held his beer to his lips as he watched her drop another bucket of beers at the corner booth. Her long, toned legs flexed as she leaned forward. Her shorts barely covered that spot where the curve of her bottom met the back of her thigh. If he wasn't so suspicious of the guys at that table, he might have bought them another round just so he could watch Liv stretch and lean again.

"Well, thank you, darlin'," Brody heard one say.

"That's mighty kind of you."

For a moment, Brody thought perhaps he'd judged them prematurely. It wouldn't have been the first time he'd allowed his jealous tendencies to bring out the worst in him. The last time it happened, he'd ended up spending the night in jail for disorderly conduct. He'd never forget that awful night. He only wished the folks of Meeteetse would.

No sooner had Brody given those boys the benefit of the doubt than one of them reached around and slapped her on the behind. When she scowled at him, the man laughed and pulled her onto his lap.

Liv shrieked in surprise and writhed to escape him. Brody flipped his lid and lunged from his chair without hesitation. He gritted his teeth. Spots blurred his vision. He was going to kill that sonofabitch.

Liv saw Brody stalking forward. She froze. She looked more frightened than the two guys who tried to warn their friend. Upping the effort, she threw an elbow into the man's chest and slipped from his grasp. "Galven, wait!" she said, throwing herself at Brody. "Listen to me. He isn't worth it." She frantically pointed toward the bar behind him. "See, Jethro's coming. He'll throw them out, and they won't be allowed back. Please, Brody, listen to me. Don't do this."

Brody could hear Liv pleading, but nothing registered. He moved her aside and barreled forward. All three guys had squeezed out of the booth, securing their spot in a defensive triangle. The biggest of the three stood in the front.

Brody scoffed, unimpressed with any of them. "I don't know where you're from, but around here, we treat women with respect."

The entire bar fell silent. No one dared to move a muscle with Brody cocked and loaded.

"You don't want to mess with me," the stranger stated, crossing his arms. "I'll have you know my father is the—"

"I don't care who your sperm donor is," Brody interrupted. "Apologize to her."

Brody felt Liv's hand on his shoulder. "It—it's okay."

"No, it isn't." Brody stared the man down. "Apologize. Now."

One of the three muttered to the guy in front, "Apologize already so we can get the hell out of here, Carlton."

"Your friend's a smart man," Brody added. "You should listen to him."

Carlton shook his head. "I don't have to listen to you or anybody in this Podunk town. And I sure as hell don't need to apologize to a *waitress*. It's her job to serve me. Besides, I think she liked having a *real* man's arms around her for a change." He leaned forward and looked Brody in the eyes. "What do you think about that? *Hillbilly*."

Brody reared back and threw the first punch, knocking Carlton and his high-dollar hat into next Sunday. His two friends caught and steadied him, aghast at the blood spewing from Carlton's nose. Carlton shook the dizziness from his brain and sprang forward only to find himself in Brody's clutches again. From there, Brody tossed him headfirst across the table, knocking beer bottles and aluminum buckets on the floor. Glass shattered at his feet as he took hold of Carlton's shirt collar and lifted him upright for another go-round.

A horrendous commotion filled the bar as every able man jumped in to pull them apart.

"Hey, hey, hey, bro! That's enough!"

Brody heard Rod's voice amid all the chaos and felt a multitude of hands clutching his shoulders and arms. He looked in the eyes of his older brother and huffed like a freight train.

Clouded by rage, he had a difficult time understanding how Rod had come to be there in the first place. He glared at his brother, then at the many hands upon him.

"Calm down, brother," Rod said, righting Brody's hat, which had shifted off-center. He gave his left cheek a brotherly pat. "You're good. You got this."

Brody shook everyone off and shoved Rod backward.

"Get off me!"

Rod stepped forward and didn't back down. "Enough. You're scaring the good people of Meeteetse here. Settle down. Take a breath. Get your bearings. It's over."

Brody drew in a long, steady breath and blew it out, glowering at Rod for getting involved. This wasn't his fight, nor did he have a clue what had gone on.

"Stay out of this, Rod."

"I can't do that, and you know it. You're my brother, and I'm not going to let you do something you'll regret later."

"Regret?" Brody almost laughed. "The only thing I regret is that I didn't throw this lowlife out the minute he sat down."

"Actually, it's not your decision who stays or goes, Brody. That would be my say."

Slowly and very meticulously, Brody turned his head until he found Jethro. He knew even before he laid eyes on him that the bar owner had made the comment. He was the one who had pressed charges against Brody years ago for a fight he didn't start. "Are you taking up for this asshole too? Did you not see what he did to Ms. Langston?"

Jethro splayed his hands in front of him and swallowed hard. "All I know is, I got one hell of a mess to clean up because you decided to take matters into your own hands. Again."

"Yeah, well, I didn't see you doing anything to help her. Is that how you treat your female employees? Turn a blind eye to gross sexual assault?"

To everyone's surprise, Carlton finally spoke up in his defense as he swiped his bloody nose across his sleeve. "Hey, hey, look, I didn't sexually assault anyone. All I did was have a little fun. Right, doll?"

Brody swiveled around and pointed at Carlton over Rod's shoulder. "You shut your mouth!"

"Brody, cool it," Rod cautioned.

"Not until he apologizes to Liv."

"Like I said," Carlton piped up again, making sure

there was enough blood on his sleeve for evidence. "I'm not apologizing to anyone. Unless you want to defend your own assault charge, Hillbilly, you might want to apologize to *me*."

"Why, you no good, motherfu—"

This time, Rod had to use all his strength to hold Brody back. Carlton staggered backward, clearly fearing for his life. Jethro stepped in, probably fearing a lawsuit. "Rod, get your brother out of here before he gets me sued."

Chapter Three

Brody stumbled out the door and into the parking lot with his brother on his heels. Rod shoved him with each step, ushering him farther from the bar until they reached Brody's vehicle.

"You want to explain what the hell happened in there?"

Brody leaned his forearms on the bed of his truck and caught his breath. He couldn't blame his brother for throwing him out of the Wagon Wheel. He knew Rod only wanted what was best for him and didn't want to see him in trouble with the law again.

On the flip side, he was mad as hell at him for it. Rod had made a complete fool out of him in front of everyone, not to mention that city slicker, Carlton. He recalled those in the bar who remembered his days of being a nuisance teen and how disappointed they looked at him now. He hated that the folks of Meeteetse still saw him that way, but he was only trying to do what was right. Surely, they'd agree that no woman should be treated that way. Maybe they hadn't seen what happened to her. Maybe they thought he was trying to start trouble again.

"Well?" Rod asked, smacking Brody upside the head.

Brody caught Rod's wrist and threw his brother's hand back at him. "I was trying to get the guy to apologize to Liv. He refused. He mouthed off. I got mad."

"Yeah, yeah, yeah. Same old story, Brody. When are you going to learn that you can't fix everything with your fists?"

"You saw him, Rod. There's no talking to guys like him."

"And there's no talking to guys like you either. All you want to do is pound someone in the ground. Over what? A girl you've got the hots for but don't have the guts to tell her?"

Brody quickly scanned the parking lot and the front porch of the bar for Liv, hoping she wasn't around to hear their conversation. "Will you shut your mouth, Rod? She can't know how I feel."

"Why? Why won't you tell her? I don't get it."

"It's not for you to understand. It's how I feel. It's my prerogative. Not yours."

Rod removed his cowboy hat and ran his hand through his hair, pacing between the vehicles. "That may be so, Brody, but you've got to pull it together. If you don't have the nerve to make a move on Olivia, then you can't get mad at every dude who does."

"The douchebag slapped her on the ass and practically shoved his hand between her legs, Rod!"

"Every red-blooded male in Meeteetse wants to. Including you."

Brody launched himself at Rod, grabbing his brother by the shirt. "Don't talk like that about Liv."

Rod chuckled in Brody's face. "See? There you go again. Defending her as if she's yours. Protecting her like you're her knight in shining armor." Rod broke away from his brother's hold and poked Brody's chest. "What are you going to do when she falls in love with someone one day? Hmm? What are you going to do when that someone isn't *you*? You going to kick his ass? Bloody his nose? Go to jail—again? 'Cause that's what's going to happen. One of these days you're going to wind up back in jail because of your temper. And this time it'll be because you messed with the wrong guy." Rod pointed toward the bar. "Like that guy in there who has connections. Who has weight behind his daddy's name, who can get charges to stick. Is that what you want?"

"No. But I'd do it. For her."

Rod scoffed. "You'd do time for her?"

Brody smirked at his brother, knowing he was only trying to get to him. "I'm not afraid, if that's what you're asking."

"You're not afraid because there's always been someone to bail you out. Always been someone in Meeteetse who knows and pities Mama for the hell she's been through since Daddy died. Always been someone who'll come to your rescue because they're hoping maybe this time you'll change."

Brody looked out at the distant Absaroka Mountains. The wide, majestic, snow-capped range reminded him of the times he and his father went fishing in the Greybull River. A time when he remembered being happy. A time when there wasn't such a thing as a huge chasm within his family.

Since his father's passing, Rod had stepped in to fill the void and take care of things as the man of the household, including watching out for Brody. He knew Rod made it his responsibility to keep him on the straight and narrow.

"You don't have to watch out for me anymore. I'm a grown man."

"Well, I've got news for you, Brody. One of these days, I'm not going to be around to save you. Or maybe one day…I just decide you're not worth saving."

Rod could've hacked him with a chainsaw and it would've hurt less. The wound his hurtful words left behind gaped open and left him to stand there weak and speechless.

Olivia called Brody's name, and, until that moment, he'd had no idea she had stepped outside. Her pace quickened once she located him in the gravel lot with Rod. Her face was full of concern and questions that he wasn't ready to address.

He drew in a much-needed breath and cleared his foggy brain. He needed to get away. To be alone with his thoughts. To distance himself from the righteous brother who cast a shadow too large for Brody to be seen.

Without so much as a good-bye, Brody ducked around

his truck and climbed inside. Unable to face Liv, he turned the key. From his peripheral vision, she laid her palms on his passenger-side window and rapped on it.

"Where are you going?"

Without even glancing her way, Brody knew there was panic in her eyes as she looked to his brother for answers.

"Rod, where's Brody going?"

Rod pulled her out of harm's way as Brody revved the engine. "He's all right. He just needs some space."

Brody's jaw hurt from grinding his teeth so hard. He threw the shifter into drive and pulled out, leaving a wake of dust behind him.

* * * *

Olivia stormed back inside the bar, and a wall of curious faces met her, none of which she acknowledged. The only person she did talk to was Jethro, her boss. She watched him sweep up the last of the glass around the corner booth before divulging her plans.

"I have to leave."

Jethro's eyes widened in surprise. "You can't leave. You're still on the clock."

"Then I'm taking myself off. Besides, you kicked my ride home out of the bar, remember? Now all I have is Rod." She glanced at the clock on the wall. "You have an hour and a half before closing. Surely, you can fill a few drink orders."

On a mission, she turned to collect her purse from the kitchen and almost ran into the three strangers coming out of the restroom. She stopped mid-stride, uncertain what to say. Her moral upbringing reminded her to say *Excuse me*, while her impulsive resentful side wanted to impart a good old-fashioned *F you*.

Carlton had obviously cleaned himself up, save for the bright red bloodstain on the sleeve of his white shirt. His cowboy hat, once pressed with clean, smooth, symmetrical ridges, had dents and arcs in random places, making it appear lopsided on his head.

Olivia bit back a smile and circled them without saying a word. When she waltzed back into the dining area, she couldn't help but notice that Carlton and his friends had found a seat at a different booth, with another round of beers, only this time they were in cold, frosty mugs. Probably on the house.

Liv seethed. She wasn't sure who she should be angrier with, Jethro for allowing them to stay, or the guys who thought they were welcome to after the ruckus they'd caused.

Rod stepped inside the bar and must have noticed the same thing. Olivia saw his forehead furrow a bit over the whole scene and wondered if he were going to call attention to it. He had as much muscle as Brody to back up his dissatisfaction and a lot more clout with the folks of this small town. If anyone could get these guys thrown out without much dispute, it was Rod. To her disappointment, he shrugged it off.

"You ready?" he murmured, crossing his arms.

She was ready, all right. Ready to make a stand. She had no idea where she'd gotten her sudden shot of fearlessness, but it hit her like a bolt of lightning. "One second, Rod." She slapped her purse against his chest and stomped toward their booth.

A sweet, bright smile split Olivia's lips as she regarded their uneasy glances. "You boys need anything else before I leave?"

Carlton smiled and set down his beer. He cleared his throat and, like the snake he was, slithered into that fake charming demeanor he'd used moments before he got his ass handed to him. "I don't believe we do, darlin'." He surveyed her up and down as if she were on the menu.

Olivia kept her cool and charmed him right back. "Wonderful. Then have a great evening." With that, she reached across the table and grabbed all three mugs by their handles, busing in one fell swoop.

"Hey, hey, hey there. What do you think you're

doing?"

"I'm sorry," Olivia simpered, glancing at the three full beer mugs in her possession and back at Carlton. "Did you still want these?"

Carlton smirked at her as if she were an idiot. "Well, yeah..." He had the earmarks of a genuine know-it-all as he remarked behind the shield of his hand, "They don't make 'em too bright up here, do they?"

Olivia flashed the biggest self-satisfied smile and poured all three mugs into Carlton's lap. Carlton jumped up, his crotch soaking wet. "What the hell? You just poured beer all over me!"

"Wow, look who the bright one is now," Olivia jeered. She saw Rod finally making his way toward the booth. "You think this guy's smart enough to know when he's outworn his welcome?"

Carlton backed up, putting some space between him and Rod. He searched the bar, hoping he'd snag just a notion of pity from someone—anyone. But every individual in the Wagon Wheel stared at him with stoic, unsympathetic eyes. Even Jethro seemed reluctant to jump on his bandwagon.

Mrs. Corinth, with her crochet needle and yarn, slipped off her barstool and stepped forward, aligning herself with Olivia. "Young man, I think it's time for you and your friends to go home. Rod? Will you kindly finish what your brother started and show these gentlemen to the door?"

"My pleasure, ma'am." Rod straightened his hat and angled his body toward the door, extending his hand. "This way, boys."

Carlton and his friends wasted no time leaving. Like reprimanded puppies, they scurried out the door and shuffled across the parking lot to their tinted-windowed, white diamond Escalade.

Olivia watched out the window until the luxury utility vehicle pulled onto the road before hugging Mrs. Corinth. She thanked the seventy-year-old woman for speaking up, wishing the rest of the people in the bar would've done the same for Brody. He was the one who deserved the support.

As she snatched her purse from Rod's hand, she smacked his arm with it. "You owe your brother an apology. You know that, right?"

Rod shook his head as he held the door open for her. "I guess I'm going to find out all about why on the way, ain't I?"

"And then some."

Chapter Four

Olivia opened the door to Rod's Chevy pickup and looked at him from the passenger seat. "Are you sure Brody's here?"

"I know my brother. Whenever he's mad, this is where he comes to blow off a little steam. Trust me."

"I know this is where he normally hides out, Rod. This ain't my first rodeo. But I don't see his truck."

"Check the woodshed." He pointed out his window toward the other side of the barn.

Olivia nodded and thanked him for the lift, hopping out of his vehicle. The sound of gravel crunched under her boots, cutting the quiet stillness of the evening. With the time being close to nine-thirty, she felt uneasy wandering around the McKinley ranch in the dark. She hoped she wouldn't end up disturbing them.

Jonas McKinley, a third generation farmer, was a handsome thirty-something-year-old who'd owned the ranch since his father died about ten years ago. His girlfriend, Ava Wallace, lived with him in the single-story log cabin, and they ran the farm together. From the talk of the town, Olivia often heard they made a decent living. Jonas and his friend, Cole Forester, took care of the cattle end of the business, while Ava managed the public trail riding tours. Each had their own set of employees to help with the daily chores. Rod and Brody were Jonas's workers, but every now and again, Brody would talk about how he'd have to step in as a trail guide for Ava when one of her girls called in sick.

Brody was the jack-of-all-trades kind of guy, able to do just about anything. Rod, on the other hand, didn't like to stray from the usual tasks. Olivia assumed it had a lot to do with the fact that Rod was the eldest. His seniority had given him the opportunity to decline the duties he didn't care for, which forced Brody to take them on instead.

Not having to fight for control was one thing Oliva liked about being an only child. And Brody's indifference was probably what had drawn her to him in the first place. He was easier to get along with than his bossy older brother and, though Rod would argue otherwise, Brody was less dramatic. Sometimes Olivia felt that if it weren't for Rod stepping in, Brody wouldn't have to prove himself all the time.

Olivia watched as Rod drove down the long gravel lane and inwardly cursed him for not sticking around to help her find his brother. Though she'd said her piece to him on the way there, Rod didn't seem to agree with her. He told her he knew his brother better than anyone and that Brody had a lot of growing up to do. He even went so far as to state that her perpetual support of Brody only encouraged his immature behavior and that he'd never learn to be a real man if she continued to coddle him.

As the red glow of taillights faded into the night, she flipped Rod the bird. No matter what Rod said, Brody was the more chivalrous brother in her eyes.

She rubbed her arms, feeling the chill of the night. Goose bumps spread like a California wildfire across her bare skin, and she wished she'd worn jeans to work instead of shorts.

She glanced up. Nearly full, the moon hung high in the sky, a silent watchman over the peaceful valley below. Only the moon and God knew how she truly felt about Brody, and she reckoned it would stay that way. Brody never gave her the impression he wanted more than her friendship. They'd grown so close through the years that now she figured she was more like a sister to him. He never said as much, but she knew. Call it woman's intuition.

Olivia exhaled, blowing out her frustrations, and regarded the many buildings that surrounded her. She'd been to the McKinley ranch before, but never in the dark.

To the northeast, at the base of a bluff, sat Jonas's log home with a wraparound porch. Soft, warm light from the front window illuminated the backs of two rocking chairs and a small table. Olivia imagined Jonas and Ava spending quiet evenings on the porch, sipping ice tea and listening to the crickets and frogs. She then contemplated that it might have been the very reason she hardly ever saw them at the Wagon Wheel. If she had a porch like that, she probably wouldn't venture out much either.

Across from the house was a dry lot, which then fed into a maze of pastures at the base of the Absaroka Mountains. According to Brody, Jonas McKinley owned some of the most beautiful acreage in the Bighorn Basin, encompassed by miles of blackboard fence.

Next to the dry lot stood a huge barn, a covered manure pit, a rock smokehouse, and a wood building with tiny fissures of light shining through each of the vertical slats. She assumed it to be the woodshed Rod had indicated, but in the dark, everything looked indistinguishable. The only thing that wasn't ambiguous was the smell of manure, hay, and dirt.

Though a little nervous to do so, Olivia proceeded forward. Dark shadows draped every recess and corner. Not a single light illuminated the grounds around the buildings, save for the moon. Taking a shot in the dark, she whispered Brody's name.

An outbreak of nickers and snorts erupted from inside the barn. Olivia bit her lip and swiveled her gaze toward the McKinley house, fearing Jonas might wander out with his gun.

"Is that you, Liv?"

Olivia yelped, whirling from the voice behind her. From out of the shadows, she saw Brody holding a hatchet. "Sonofabitch, Galven! You nearly gave me a heart attack." She pressed her hand to her heart and gasped for breath.

"What are you doing here?" he asked.

"What the hell are you doing with an ax?"

"Splitting wood."

"At this hour? Are you crazy?"

"There's light in the shed. And you still haven't answered *my* question."

"I came to see you." She struggled with how to explain herself without making it sound as if she were checking up on him. "To see if you needed any company."

He peered beyond her toward the driveway. "And I reckon Rod dropped you off?"

She walked toward him, hoping to see his facial expressions more clearly before she answered. "I asked him to."

Brody's head fell back, and he inhaled deeply. He looked irritated. "Aren't you supposed to be working?"

"I clocked out. And most everyone was fixing to leave anyway."

"And Jethro was okay with that?"

"What's he going to do? Fire me?" She tried to get Brody to laugh. He didn't. Instead, he crossed his arms.

"He very well could fire you."

Olivia scoffed. "He'd have to grow a set first."

This time Brody harrumphed. At least she was able to pull something from him. Past experience reminded her it wasn't going to be easy to connect with Brody. Getting him to open up would be like prying a walnut from its shell. Determined to try, she sidled up to him and reached for his hand.

He stepped away. "Look, I'm not sure why you came here tonight, Liv, but I don't really feel like talking."

Unsure what to do with her outstretched hand, Olivia tucked it under her pit and crossed her arms. "Okay. So, don't talk. I'll just watch you split wood. Besides, you're kind of my ride home now."

Brody glanced down the gravel drive and grimaced. "Right."

He sighed and walked back into the shadows between the buildings. Liv followed him, tripping on high grass and anything else she couldn't see. The strong scent of dung

71

smacked her in the face as she passed the manure pit and turned the corner. His truck came into view first, parked perpendicular to the woodshed with the tailgate down. On it sat a cooler and two empty bottles of beer.

The shed was a three-sided building with an open front and a lean-to porch extending from the roof. In this way, wood could be split, loaded up, hauled out, or stacked inside while out of the elements.

With plenty of room to move, Brody stepped over a haphazard heap of split wood on the ground and reached inside the cooler on his tailgate. "You want one?"

Olivia joined him and leaned against his truck. She glanced at the ax he placed on the bed and frowned inwardly. "Sure."

He twisted off the top and handed it to her before resuming his work. She took a sip, observing him as he grabbed armfuls of wood and added them to a large stack against the back wall. It worried her that he'd wielded a sharp blade under the influence of alcohol. Stupid, really.

Given Brody's current state of mind, she figured she'd board that train from a different station. "So, Jonas is okay with you coming to his ranch and hanging out?"

"Why would he care?"

"I don't know." Olivia shrugged. "Because it's late. And you're on his property. Isn't that a legal risk for him if something happened?"

Brody gauged her question as he lugged another armload. "I'd never sue Jonas. He's the only one in this town who doesn't look at me like I'm some worthless convict."

She felt the tender eggshells cracking beneath her feet. "Sure, but Jonas doesn't know if you're a sue-happy kinda guy. Nor could he guarantee—"

"Liv," Brody cut her off, his hands on his hips now. "I know what you're thinking, but for your information, I didn't drink a single beer while I split wood. And the two you see empty are from when I saw Rod pull up. I tossed them back thinking I was about to get another ass chewing.

So there. Happy now?"

"Not really."

"Well, then, I don't know what to tell you. I can't fix everything for you, Liv."

Chapter Five

Brody didn't mean to lash out. When it came to Liv, he normally watched his mouth and minded his manners. Tonight, he didn't have much control over his behavior. He sighed and hung his head. "I'm sorry."

He blamed it on his brother. Rod had stuck his nose in where it didn't belong, and Rod sure as hell hadn't done him any favors by breaking up the fight. It would've been different if Rod had kicked the guys out right after he and Carlton were separated. At least it would've conveyed the notion that Rod had his back. Instead, Rod made him look like a complete fool.

Brody closed his eyes, feeling his blood begin to boil again. Splitting wood had always helped him take the edge off, but what he wouldn't give for a good old-fashioned punching bag right now.

Liv put down her beer and came to him. She stroked his forearm, trying to ease his tension. She knew him well. So much so that she monitored his clenched fists—fists he hadn't even realized he'd made until now.

He felt her fingers stroke the inside of his wrist before she clasped her hand around his. She lifted his right one and inspected the cut on his knuckle. "You don't have to apologize, Galven. I know exactly why you're mad. I'd be mad too." She ran her finger along the swelling of the laceration. "Is this from the fight?"

He loved her touch. The cool sensation of her fingertips on his hot skin whittled away his resolve. "Mm-hmm."

"I never thanked you for coming to my rescue."

He'd do it again if he had to. "You don't have to thank

me." His voice came out strained and hoarse.

"I know you don't need my gratitude, but you deserve it."

She bent and placed a kiss upon his busted knuckle. He clenched his jaw to trap a groan. The feel of her lips brushing his skin damn near socked him in the gut. He'd taken hard blows in the stomach many times before, but nothing compared to this.

His brain automatically painted a picture of Liv's soft lips leaving a trail of kisses up his arm, across his collarbone, and up his neck until she reached his mouth. He envisioned her lips on his and her hands in his hair, pulling him into a deeper, passionate kiss.

On weak legs, he stepped back and bumped into the wall behind him.

Liv gawked at him, confused by his sudden need to flee. Her perplexity then turned to despair. "Does the thought of me gross you out that much, Galven?"

She waited for an answer, but he couldn't provide one. Nothing could've been further from the truth.

When he didn't reply, frustration scrunched her face and she heaved a sigh. "I'll just call Rod."

She turned and headed out of the woodshed. Brody leapt forward and caught her wrist. "Liv, wait."

He spun her around and studied the hurt in her eyes. To the average Joe, there was no evidence of pain, not even a single tear. But he knew better. The sting of rejection was there. "It's not that you gross me out."

Her brow cocked upward as she stared at her feet. He sensed her doubt.

"I was surprised, is all. You kind of caught me off guard."

She couldn't seem to look him in the eye. Why did he have to hurt her?

"Liv, please."

Her gaze slowly found his. He couldn't read her. Maybe she *did* want him the way he wanted her. Perhaps she had found the courage to let him know how she felt by initiating a heartfelt, uncomplicated kiss and he had to go and shoot her down. Or maybe he was hooked so deep on a wish that he blew every little thing she did out of proportion.

"Galven?"

He swallowed hard, trying to stay strong. He had to. For her sake. He couldn't give her a reason to hang back in Meeteetse if the call from Nashville came. Regardless of how bad she wanted it, Liv would put her dreams on hold for those she cared about, and he'd never forgive himself if he became that person.

As hard as he tried, the idea of coming clean tempted him. He could think of nothing else but blurting it out and letting the chips fall where they may. He wanted her to know exactly how he felt, to prove it with a long, hot, passionate kiss.

He could see himself picking her up in his arms and laying her down in the back seat of his truck. The sound of his name on her lips would quake the ground harder than any rumble of thunder.

Only she could truly relieve this awful pain in his heart.

"Liv, I… I need to tell you… I mean… I want…"

"Yes?" she encouraged.

Her tantalizing bottom lip distracted him. He tried again. "I want you." As soon as it rolled off his tongue, he regretted it. He sounded selfish and stupid. He couldn't do this to her. "I want you…to go for a drive with me."

She blinked repeatedly. "A drive?"

He exhaled in relief. "Yeah. A drive. Over the ridge. There's this place on Jonas's farm where you can look out over the valley. And sometimes, if the moon hangs right, you can see its reflection in the Upper Sunshine Reservoir. Wanna go?"

"Right now?"

"Why not? It's a gorgeous night."

Another bout of confusion manifested on Liv's face. "What about the rest of this wood?"

A slew of erection jokes he'd never be able to share

bounced around in his head. "I'll finish tomorrow morning. Come on."

He grabbed the ax with one hand and swung it, burying its blade in the broad side of one of the logs. He then made quick work of his tailgate, cleaning it off and pushing back the cooler so he could close it. Together, they climbed in the truck and drove across the field to the east gate.

Brody opened and closed several gates before they reached their destination, all the while feeling Liv's thigh brushing against his as they bounced in the seat. The drive there was not a quick one, but it sure made for an adventure. Many times, Liv squealed in excitement and steadied her beer so it wouldn't spill when they bounded across ruts and bumps in the fields. He could admit to sometimes hitting them on purpose in order to throw her against him and hear her laughter. Her hand, braced on his thigh, wasn't bad either.

After pulling through and closing the last gate, he eased his truck along the pasture grass so as not to damage it. Sleepy steers, huddled in groups, stared at them as they passed by.

Liv sat up straighter and gazed out the rear window. "Oh my gosh, they're following us."

"That's because they think they're getting fed. They associate a pickup truck with buckets of grain."

Brody steered his Chevy along the fence and crested the hill. He threw it in park beneath a large oak and killed the engine. Liv swiveled in her seat, and her mouth gaped in awe at the view before her.

Like a page out of a vacation destination magazine, a breathtaking display of peaks and meadows, veiled with pines and firs, stretched for miles. A shimmering mirror of moonlit water lay tucked in a valley of hills. Beyond that rose the majestic Absaroka mountain range beneath a sea of twinkling stars in a midnight sky.

"Oh my gosh, Galven. This is amazing!"

She handed him her beer and inched to the edge of the

seat. Her palm came down on his leg again as she pushed herself closer to the windshield. Any man with a working nervous system would stir at the feel of a woman's hand on his thigh. He was no different.

He doused the fire in his soul with a swig of her beer. *God, help me.*

"Brody, I can't believe how gorgeous this is."

"I know," he concurred, though his eyes weren't fixed on the scenery outside his truck. The view from the inside was a thousand times better.

Without tearing away her gaze, Liv leaned back and nestled herself against his chest. Brody hesitated but eventually threw an arm over her and pulled her close. The feel of her body pressed against his did little to ease the turbulence of his thoughts. From wondering if he reeked of perspiration to praying he'd have the strength to resist the urge of kissing her again, he couldn't relax.

"Brody?" she commenced.

He swallowed. "Yeah?"

"Do you ever stop and think where we'll be five years from now? Like if we'll still be doing the same old things we do now?"

He wasn't sure where she was going with this. "Meaning…"

"Meaning, if you'll still be working here and me at the Wagon Wheel." She reached over and took the beer from his hand, tipping it to her lips. "I don't want to be a waitress for the rest of my life."

Brody heard the despondence in her voice and manned up. "You know what I think?"

She rotated her head to meet his gaze. "What?"

He smoothed her hair away from her forehead and admired her rare beauty. He stroked the flawless skin on her face and even though her sweet, supple lips dared him to capture them in a kiss, it occurred to him that he might never get an opportunity kiss her ever again should she jet off to Nashville.

Ignoring every compulsion he had to do just that, he

simply offered a smile. "I think that call you've been waiting for is gonna come in sooner than you think."

Liv sighed and sank back into his torso, her hand resting on his chest. "I don't know about that. I mean, I've been working hard to get a website up and running. And I have a Facebook page like my agent insisted. I've even recorded a few songs on YouTube to get some exposure while she supposedly works her magic with the record-label bigwigs. I just want this so bad, Galven, I can taste it."

Brody considered Liv's words and the earnest desire she had to see her dream come true. He respected how hard she worked to get her foot in the door and that she wasn't content to sit by and wait for something to happen. Whether it be by accident or by the connections of her agent, Olivia Langston was going to be a country music superstar. He knew it. As sure as eggs, he knew it.

Brody let his head fall back against the rear window and cast a glance outside his truck, staring at nothing in particular. The things she worried about were a far cry from what troubled him.

Liv thought of what she'd do if that call *never* came.

He worried about what he'd do when it did.

Just the thought of letting her go pierced his heart like a hard-driven horseshoe nail.

He closed his eyes and propelled those gloomy thoughts from his mind. Until the day when he'd have to say good-bye, he'd treasure every moment with her and be the man she needed him to be.

He glanced at Liv, all snuggled against his chest, and smiled. For now, what she needed from him seemed to be just a friend to lean on.

Something's Bound To Happen

Jamett & Joseph Series

Chapter One

"You're such a jerk!"

The malicious tone and volume of a woman's complaint caused my head to turn in the direction of the chaos a few doors down the hall of my apartment complex. After whipping her scarf around her neck in finality, the angered woman marched down the corridor. A man, who I assume was the jerk in question, pursued her. At this moment, I realized their argument was not meant for my eyes or ears. The guy showed up for the fight in nothing but a towel. His bare chest and arms boasted the remnants of a golden summer tan, even in late November.

I rolled my eyes. How was it possible that men still looked divine in winter, while we women have to make an occasional visit to the tanning salon so we don't appear pasty white? Sure, some of us tried rockin' the pale skin look of the Twilight vampire craze, but it never seemed to catch on with the male population. They still preferred their women toned and tanned. Realize, this was merely my conclusion given no man had yet to fall head over heels for me.

"How can I be a jerk for trying to help you forget about your horrible day?" he asked, grasping the woman's arm and tugging her back. Thankfully, he was oblivious to me standing three doors down.

"No, you're a jerk because *you* tried to forget about *my* horrible day by coming on to me," the girl corrected.

The woman then looked past the man's shoulders and suddenly took notice of my presence. The minute our eyes met, heat flushed my entire body. I quickly averted my attention and pretended not to notice their public tiff, fiddling with my keys to find the right one for locking up. I didn't know what angered her more—the fact that I had taken an interest in their argument or that I had seen her boyfriend in a state of near nakedness.

I half expected her to call me out. Instead, she went back to berating the guy. From where I stood, I had established him as a normal, sexually-active (given he came on to her), heterosexual male. It also bears mentioning that he looked very fine in his bathroom apparel.

"I came to you because I needed you, Joseph."

Ah, the jerk in the towel had a name. Not sure why I made a mental note of it, but I did.

"And I'm still here," he concluded, spreading his arms wide. "You're the one who's leaving."

Clearly, the man was not in tune with the proverbial emotional needs of modern day women. If I were keeping score, he'd have lost a point for that little sarcastic remark. However, his choice of morning attire kept the tally in his favor.

"You just don't get it, do you?" she barked back, slamming her hands upon her hips. "You think everything can be solved with a song or sex."

A song? Now this just got a little more interesting.

"You didn't like what I wrote?" he asked.

With my eyes still buried in the ring of keys clutched in my gloved hands, I couldn't help but notice the slight hint of sadness in Joseph's voice. My heart longed to sneak a peek at him, another potential point in his favor should I see a pitiful expression of pain in his face. But the girl's harsh reaction forbade me to even try a nonchalant glance his way.

"Oh, don't you dare! Don't you dare turn this around and make me the bad guy."

Okay, I was weak. I couldn't help it. I had to catch a glimpse of what was to come. I inserted the correct key into the lock of my apartment door and peered out of the corner of my eye. She poked him in the chest. Repeatedly.

"Again, this is why you are a jerk. You think the world revolves around you and that you play no part in its destruction when it's crumbling around you. You're above it all, yet so far up its ass you can't see the light of day."

He didn't budge or even stop her finger-poke punishment. He stared at her, stunned. "I can't believe you didn't like the song. I was up all night. I wrote that for *you*, Caroline."

My eyes grew wide of their own volition. A songwriter? My sexy, half-dressed, James Tudor underwear model-like neighbor was a songwriter? My heart melted as I stood there. I imagined this man—yes…he was still sporting the towel—hunkered down over a well-worn set of piano keys, pounding out words of love and emotion with each lyrical stanza, every consecutive note inspired by the last. In my mind, I stood tall and proud, holding a white square sign with a bold, black, number ten on it above my head. Fireworks went off behind me in the distance, and a fluttering cloud of confetti fell around me.

This guy is a keeper!

I wanted to run up and give him a congratulatory hug on his big win, but the girlfriend—or soon-to-be-ex-girlfriend, if all of my assumptions were on the money—rolled her eyes and turned her back to him.

"You were never cut out to be a songwriter, Joseph. Just like you, your music lacks heart."

She left him standing in the narrow hallway, injured and bleeding. The knife in his chest remained at such a vicious angle that I began to wonder if he'd ever live through it. If it were me, I would have been crushed to the core. Then again, I wouldn't have settled for someone like her. I would have been smart enough to keep my standards raised and my heart better guarded.

Inwardly, I sighed. I supposed it was easier for me to say those things when I was outside looking in. I shouldn't have been listening in the first place. That's when my brain kicked into panic overdrive.

If he turned around right now, he'd see that I'd partaken in being a rude onlooker with a front row seat to his pathetic break-up. And I'd no longer be the cute, little neighbor who he—hypothetically speaking—might run into one day because he wasn't watching where he was going as he walked down the hall. He wouldn't suddenly feel compelled to ask me out on a date because he was a hopeless romantic and believed wholeheartedly in love at first sight. And fate. Surely fate had a part in all this.

My mind raced as I continued to stand there like a deer in headlights, freaking out over the moment when he'd give up staring down the hall and turn toward his door. If I made a break for the elevator, he'd see me do so. If I stayed where I was, he'd still see me. No matter what I decided, I was doomed to be caught eavesdropping.

Considering the perilous situation I was in, one would think I wouldn't dare take one more peek down the hall. But I did.

My terrycloth-kilted neighbor ran frustrated fingers through his dark, nigh-in-need-of-a-cut hair and, just as I feared, turned around.

I don't know who was more shocked, him or me. It was evident he hadn't expected to see anyone in the hall, much less a pale, brunette with barely a curve to her body, all of which were hidden behind a fluffy winter parka, scarf, and gloves.

I stared, frozen in my boots, my eyes bulging from their sockets. He returned the same stunned look. For a split second, I thought I saw the corners of his mouth twitch upward in a smile. So, I smiled back out of courtesy.

Short-lived as that thought was, his brow furrowed. He glanced back over his shoulder as if gathering his bearings on where he and his girlfriend had chosen to have their dispute and determining whether it were possible I witnessed it all from where I stood. I could have sworn I saw a hint of embarrassment on his face as he scratched his head. "Did you...I mean, did we disturb you? Could you actually hear us from inside?"

"Oh, no," I tried to explain at the same time I aimed to comfort him. "You didn't disturb me. I was out here the whole time." I clamped my mouth shut. I had just blatantly admitted to eavesdropping on his personal conversation.

He eyes widened, and his chin tilted upward a bit. "Really..."

"I-I mean, not the whole time, just...well...."

It was my turn to be embarrassed, and I squeezed my eyes closed. Tightly. At least now, I could proudly say I was both weak and a horrible conversationalist.

Okay, you big idiot, say goodbye, cut your losses, and consider yourself lucky that he doesn't know your name. For all he knows, you're just a friend of the person who lives in Loft B and you were just leaving.

Better yet, perhaps he'll be so distraught over this whole morning that days from now when he runs into you again, as you're visiting your friend in Loft B, he won't even recognize you.

I liked the idea. So much that I'd already started plotting out my strategy. I'd donate this coat and the rest of my winter outerwear to Goodwill and buy a whole new ensemble, just in case he had a photographic memory. I'd act like we had never met and start anew.

He came closer, his eyes zeroing in on me. They rivaled the bluest Montana sky on a summer afternoon. "You're the new girl, right? You just moved in a couple weeks ago. Sutherland, is it?"

There went that plan. Wait. Did he just reveal in a very subtle, yet sly fashion that he took enough notice of me to remember my name? And *how* did he know my name? Had he broken into my mailbox and rummaged through my mail? Or worse, the dumpster?

No. I refused to believe this beautiful creature, as bold as he was talking to me in a towel, would resort to dumpster diving for any reason. Still, the question remained.

"Yeah, that's me. I'm Sutherland. Jamie Sutherland."

I had to look away. Joseph's eyes threatened to spellbind me, and I wondered how Caroline had the strength to deflect his hypnotic powers. By the looks of her glamorous appeal, I imagined she was a regular temptress herself, with the ability to stop traffic a mile away. I, on the other hand, was a plain Jane; brown hair, brown eyes, small build without a voluptuous curve in sight—the girl next door with the body of a twelve-year old boy—which was how a grudge-nursing ex-boyfriend once described me four years ago. To this day, I still choke up over his unpleasant portrayal.

"Welcome to the building, Jamie."

I dared to sneak another peek at him, hoping I could get through this conversation without looking like a faint-hearted schoolgirl. "How did you know my name?" I finally asked.

"Your name is on the mailbox for Loft B. I just put two and two together and came up with you."

It was nice to know the man knew his math. It should come in handy when he counted the reasons why he should've steered clear of me. Granted, I was not as needy as that Caroline girl, nor was I an attention-seeking drama queen. I avoided sinking to those emotional levels at all costs. I was a strong, independent woman who had no need for a man in her life. I'd tried the "couple" thing—multiple times—and I'd failed royally each go round.

Given the copious amounts of money I'd lost and the countless tears I'd shed over those "Mr. Rights" gone horribly wrong, I swore never to get sucked into the ridiculous notion of romance and all the frilly fringe benefits that supposedly came with it. I was a pessimistic woman. What I remembered most about love was not the endearing looks, warm hugs, or the cute butterflies in the stomach. It was the sucker punch in the gut when I least expected it.

"I should go," I said in haste, trying to remind myself that even this Greek Adonis-like man with kind blue eyes was capable of throwing a TKO punch.

He grinned, glanced down at his rather inappropriate attire, and thumbed over his shoulder toward his open apartment door. "Me too. Gotta get to work."

The innocence in his smile knocked me off balance. He went from bold and witty to downright adorable. It was a good thing he had already started to take a few steps backward, else I might have reached out and pinched his cute, five-o'clock-shadowed cheeks. The longer I stood here, the more I was convinced Caroline was clinically insane for going all diva on this man.

Stepping beneath his doorframe, he nodded once, reaffirming the beauty of his boyish grin, and closed the door.

A breath I had no idea I was even holding escaped me. My arms fell limp at my sides, keys rattling in my hand. I still had no grasp of what had really happened. The only thing that registered was Joseph and how he was quite possibly the best-looking jerk I'd ever seen.

Chapter Two

All the way to work, I recapped the morning.

Joseph was a healthy, heterosexual male, a songwriter, who had a steady job, or at least, I assumed he had one since he said he had to get to work—wherever that might be. He was not afraid to express his emotions, though he may have some issues with understanding and predicting the emotions of the opposite sex. A major setback as far as the female race was concerned, but I could work on that. It was fixable with the right amount of nurturing.

He was confident, bold—without the arrogance—and looked mighty fine after a shower. His eyes were blue, his lashes long, and his face chiseled. His hair hung in his face at times, but not enough to annoy me. In fact, it had taken everything I had not to thread my eager fingers through its wild softness. And the best part of all—after checking his left hand for a ring or a tell-tale tan line—Caroline was indeed just a girlfriend and not a wife.

Three hours into work, and I was still thinking of this guy. I had more pressing things to do than wonder whether I'd run into him again when I got home, like unpacking the rest of my things from my recent move. Although I wouldn't really call it a move, since I was still in the same area code as before. I'd left one apartment complex, for reasons too boring to mention, and moved into another a few blocks away.

I didn't care much for drastic changes, and I was not a wanderer. I enjoyed knowing I'd lived in the Northern Kentucky/Southern Ohio area all my life. In the last seven years of it, I owned my own little coffee shop in downtown Cincinnati called *I Like You a Latte*. It might sound like a spin-off *Starbucks*, but my little corner café offers great tasting coffee without the hefty prices.

"Can I get you anything else?" I asked routinely, before cashing the customer out. While I ran on autopilot for most of the day, my brain continued to take detours toward Destination Joseph. The view was always great, but the amount of time I spent in this one-track automobile was getting to me.

"You okay?"

I glanced in the direction of the voice and smiled. Melissa knew me better than I sometimes knew myself. I had hired her the same day she applied, assuming she would be the perfect person to help me take this pipe dream and turn it into a successful business venture. As I'd thought, she was all that and more. Melissa was not only a great employee, but also a wonderful, loyal friend.

"I'm fine," I played off, wiping spilled cream from the counter in front of the espresso machine.

Melissa stacked more cups beside the countless flavored elixir bottles. "You seem frazzled."

I wanted to laugh. Joseph had caused me to feel a lot of emotions in such a short time today, but frazzled was not one of them. I went for slightly off-kilter. "Thanks for asking, but really, I'm fine."

"Does he have a name?"

Joseph almost left my mouth before I caught on to her sly inquiry. I held my tongue and rolled my eyes. "There is no *he*. Therefore, there is no name to speak of. Good try."

Melissa gave my hip a disco bump and continued arranging the lids. "He's *that* good looking, huh?"

"I don't know what you're talking about." I tried to sound convincing, but again, I sucked at lying. The look on Melissa's face illustrated that very point. "Look," I placated, aiming for a different approach. "I just had a rough start this morning. I was up late unpacking—"

"Still?" Melissa interrupted. "I thought you said it would only take a few days."

"Yes, it would if I were in the mood to rummage through boxes of stuff I probably don't need. I already unpacked the essentials."

"So, get rid of the extra boxes. Toss them. Don't even look inside. If you haven't needed anything from them in the past two weeks, you probably can do without them altogether."

Melissa's logic sounded perfectly rational. I'd love to be able to chuck the unpacked boxes of crap and never look back. The problem was I inherited the pack rat gene. I couldn't get rid of anything. For whatever reason, I looked at my junk, even items of fad clothing and college memorabilia from fifteen years ago, and couldn't get away from this crazy idea I'd need it someday. My inability to declutter was a curse.

"I told you I'd help you," Melissa reminded me. "We could get it finished in one night."

Somehow I doubted that. Melissa, as good a friend as she was, had never seen my 'stash,' and I'd rather keep it that way. "I appreciate the offer, but I'll get it done one of these nights."

"Well, you better do it fast before this cute guy asks you out." Melissa leaned in close and spoke softly so only I could hear. "Nothing's worse than being in the middle of a hot, toe-curling kiss at the door, and you can't invite him in because there are boxes on every flat surface in your apartment." She raised her brow, hoping I caught the subtle hint.

I slapped my wet rag at her and frowned. Her attempts to get me to admit there was a man in my life were ridiculous. Joseph was not in my life. He was in my apartment building on the same floor, but nothing more. I'd hardly call our encounter in the hallway this morning an introduction to a love affair. If that were the case, I'd be having a seriously torrid affair with the teenaged dog walker who insisted on holding the lobby door open for me each evening so I could trip over five drooling hounds on tangled leashes.

"For the last time," I said, my voice taking on a strange tone of seriousness and determination. "There is no one in my life, nor is he about to ask me out. I barely know him."

"I knew it!" Melissa fist-pumped triumphantly.

Most everyone in the joint looked in my direction. I closed my eyes and hung my head.

Ignoring the weight of our customers' stares, Melissa slid closer to me. "How did you two meet? Come on, you can tell me. Is he that construction worker who whistled at you the other day from the scaffold across from *The Red Squirrel?*"

I cringed. I remembered that guy, and I wanted to elbow Melissa hard for even bringing his foul image into my head. "Eww…no."

Another idea popped into her head. Her eyes grew wide, and she almost started jumping up and down. Melissa was always an animated chatterbox. "Is he the professor from NKU who asked for directions to the Aronoff Art Center after he bought a Pumpkin Spice Latte, light on the cream, double cinnamon?"

"No, he is not. And how in the world do you remember what the professor ordered?" If I recalled correctly, he came in almost three weeks ago and hadn't been back since.

Melissa rubbed her neck nervously as if she'd suddenly developed chickenpox. "I don't know how I remember those things. But I'm glad your man is not the professor." She bit her lip. "'Cause I was hoping to get all over that the next time he comes in."

I was not surprised. Melissa always had a thing for male teachers.

"Come on, Jamett Penelope Sutherland, tell me who he is."

I glanced around, hoping no one had heard her. I gave her a strict look. "You know you're not supposed to call me by my full name. *No one* is allowed to call me that, not even my own mother who blessed me with that horrible name."

"Tell me his name, and yours shall remain…" She made a zipping-of-the-lips gesture and baited me with challenging eyes.

I knew Melissa wouldn't share my despicable secret in this blackmailing fashion, but the look on her face had me second-guessing. "I only know his first name," I confessed.

"A first name will do," she reasoned. "I can tell a lot from a man's first name."

I cocked my brow. "Like what?"

"Like if he's upstanding and intelligent versus a dimwitted louse. You know what I mean. Never will you find a man with the name of Maxwell to be an unemployed drug addict. He'd be wealthy and well mannered, unlike Willard or Clyde. You can just see the picket fence of rotten teeth and smell the stench of day-old cigarettes and Jack Daniels with those names."

"Oh my goodness," I feigned my best look of disgust and disappointment. I swallowed hard, hard enough that Melissa could see my throat bob. "His name is Clyde."

I loved the look on her face. It was priceless. Immediately, she began comforting me by rubbing my arms and adjusting her own explanation. "No, I didn't mean Clyde, I meant…" She struggled to come up with a believable name at the drop of a hat. I almost felt sorry for her.

I cracked a smile as she stuttered about, wishing I had a camera so I could capture this moment. It was not every day I could pull one over on Melissa. Eventually, she caught on to my ruse, and it was my turn to be slapped.

"Girl, I oughta…." she warned with a theatrical fist.

I couldn't help but laugh. "His name is Joseph," I surrendered, as I went over to wait on the next customer. From behind me, I could practically hear the gears churning in Melissa's head, turning the name over and over, though I hadn't expected to hear her say it aloud, pairing my name with his.

"Jamett and Joseph."

I flashed a glare over my shoulder, expressing my displeasure of her outspoken thought processes, but she paid it no heed. Instead she mouthed, "I like it," and sashayed her way to the crowded café tables.

Chapter Three

The day had been extra long. I tried to blame it on the fact that it was Friday and the last day of the sale of our seasonal Thanksgiving line of cappuccinos, but rationale told me it was because Joseph had made a lasting impression on my brain. I normally didn't get all hung up on pretty men. Truth be told, I didn't understand what made this guy so special that I'd obsess about him throughout my entire day.

Sure, I had the privilege of eyeing the man in a towel, ogling his tight little gluteus maximus without his knowledge. And I'd salivated over the view of his muscled chest just perfectly dusted with the right amount of hair as he soothed me with the sound of his deep, dulcet voice. But did that really make him worthy of taking root in my thoughts and refusing to leave?

It was kind of rude, if you asked me. I never wanted him there. Towel or no towel.

Okay, that didn't come out right. It was bad enough I had images of this man draped in nothing but soft, white terrycloth, much less introducing thoughts of removing said cloth. Not good.

I shook my head and locked my coffee shop for the night, eager to walk the streets of Cincinnati and breathe the brisk Midwest air without ruminating over Joseph.

I barely took three steps before the man invaded my thoughts again. Seriously? Was I this feeble and weak-minded that I couldn't go a single minute without fanaticizing about Joseph's body and eyes and smile and...

Yeah, I was pathetic.

Accepting myself for the pitiable excuse that I was, I walked the remaining blocks from Fountain Square to the local grocery store on Seventh Street, succumbing to the realization that Joseph, and his exquisite body, would accompany me.

* * * *

After picking up what I needed to fill my pitifully empty refrigerator—and by fill, I meant no more than I could carry on foot without my arms breaking off at the elbows—I entered my apartment complex. Somehow, I dodged the dog walker and made it to the elevator without bumping into a single person who suddenly felt compelled to welcome the new girl.

Upon stepping off, I noticed the hall was clear. No Joseph.

Just as I had this morning, I fumbled with my keys and reminded myself that before I did anything else, I would get rid of any unnecessary ones (yes, I hoard even my keys), so I wouldn't tarry at my door and run the risk of running into Joseph again.

Staying clear of Joseph was pertinent to my sanity. I was trying to forget him.

"Here, let me help you."

I jumped out of my skin at hearing someone's voice behind me. I jerked away so quickly that one of my grocery bags ripped at its bottom, sending a few canned goods to the floor with a thud and several oranges bouncing and rolling down the hall.

Immediately, I bent at the waist to retrieve the nearest oranges before they could get away. This person had the same idea. We hit heads, and I fell flat on my rump. I blinked several times so my eyes could focus. My assaulter had taken off down the hall and, to my surprise, he ran after the unruly fruit.

"I'm sorry. I'm sorry. I'm sorry. I was only trying to help you unlock your door since your hands were full."

I couldn't take my eyes off the man chasing my oranges. It was quite a sight to see. He was dressed in casual slacks, a button-up white shirt, dress shoes, and a tie. When he succeeded in apprehending the fleeing produce, he stood up with his hands above his head, holding the captive goods in a celebratory stance. "Got 'em!"

My eyes nearly popped out of my head. The savior of my rolling oranges was Joseph. I barely recognized him with his clothes on.

I scuffled to my feet, my head pounding, my mind scrambling. This was not supposed to happen. I was *supposed* to get into my apartment, unload my groceries, throw away the useless keys, and collapse in my nice comfy sleigh bed. I had so looked forward to it, and now the opportunity had slipped through my fingers. I felt like I was watching reruns of this morning's reality show. And I hate reality TV.

I grimaced as I gathered myself and my belongings, trying very hard not to look at Joseph. He picked up the ripped brown paper bag and handed it to me with a smile, probably hoping to smooth things other. I didn't return the gesture, hoping he'd kindly back away.

"I truly am sorry. Is your head all right?"

I wanted to push him away. Childish, I know, but he threatened to ruin the balance I'd come to enjoy in my solitary existence.

"Jamie?" He touched my hand, which had begun to insert the key into the doorknob. My hands were absent gloves this time, and I could feel the warmth of his palm on my wrist. Inwardly, I was thankful that I wore a huge parka, for I had hoped it was thick enough to mute the sound of my hammering heart from his ears.

Our eyes met again, and I swore I lost all feeling in my legs. The spectrum of color in his irises hypnotized me, and I couldn't break the spell.

"Are you all right?" he asked again.

I swallowed and shook off the trance he'd put me in. "Um, yeah." I resumed inserting the key into the lock, despite the pressing realization of his hand still on mine. I turned and pushed, and the door swung open.

Finally, he let go and stepped back.

"Yeah, I'm fine," I tried to smooth over the awkwardness. "I appreciate you chasing my fruit." I held up the one I had in my hand. "Orange you glad you came by when you did?"

He gave a chuckle, though I was certain he only meant to humor me. I was not that funny.

"Actually, I am glad I came by when I did."

I added charming to this guy's list of redeeming qualities. I could've added more if I wanted, but it wouldn't do me a bit of good. I refused to let myself fall for him.

Ignoring his statement and the intensity of his gaze, I entered my apartment and set the undamaged grocery bag and my purse on the entryway table. When I turned around to salvage the rest of my canned goods from the floor, I froze in my tracks. Joseph was standing in my doorway, holding the oranges as if they were objects of a truce offering, and he branded the most beautiful, honest smile I'd ever seen.

His eyes scanned over my darkened apartment. I wasn't sure what he was looking for, but I knew I wasn't ready for a man to peek into my personal space.

I grabbed the door and closed it enough that only my body could fit through, forcing him to step back into the hall. With my foot, I slid the canned goods past the threshold and confiscated the oranges from his hands.

"I'd love to stick around and chat some more," I fibbed, "but I'm…" I stumbled on my words. *What was I doing tonight?*

"Yeah, me too," he finished for me. "I've got to be somewhere…" He checked his watch, "in an hour. Big date."

Big date, huh? Even I could see he made that up so he didn't look like a pitiful schmuck with nothing to do on a Friday evening because his girlfriend had broken up with him less than twelve hours before.

Two can play this little game.

Before I knew what I was doing, I spilled forth my big imaginary plans for the night. "Yeah, I've got a big date too. He's a professional bodybuilder."

His face furrowed.

Clearly that career choice was not as awe-inspiring for Joseph as it was for me. I needed to do better. "And a doctor. Surgeon. He just does the bodybuilding on the side."

"Really," he nodded, pretending to be moved by my make-believe date's credentials. "Impressive."

"Yeah, he's always so busy, and this is the first night off he's had in months. I'm cooking a huge dinner. Candlelight."

"I see…sounds nice."

I nodded my head in time with his. We seemed to be measuring each other up, hoping to rouse some small amount of jealousy with our sorry stories. Or waiting for the other to give in and initiate the farewells. He broke first.

"Well, I don't want to hold you up."

"Thanks," I replied, starting to close the door. "And thanks again for—"

"No problem," he said, dismissing my gratitude with a wave of his hand. "If not for me, you wouldn't have lost your oranges in the first place."

His sudden change in tone pulled on my heartstrings. Yes, he was the reason my head hurt and my groceries had hit the floor, but deep down I knew his intentions were good. He was only trying to help me open my door since my hands were full, and I reacted like a skittish rabbit zigzagging in headlights.

If anything, I owed him an apology for the lies I told. Come to think of it, I told so many today that if I were made of wood, I'd put Pinocchio to shame.

Inch by inch, I closed the door. His wave goodbye was the last thing I saw before the lock clicked shut. I listened with my ear pressed against the wood until I heard his footsteps fade down the hall. Only it wasn't his door closing I heard, but the ding of the elevator.

I guess he did have plans. And I was the pathetic schmuck now.

Chapter Four

I could actually say I accomplished something tonight, besides running off the most handsome man in the Midwest. I'd sifted through my keys and thrown away the ones I didn't need. I know it may not sound like a big deal for the average unsentimental person, but for me...it was like parting with ancient family heirlooms.

My key ring now only had six keys on it—one for the security door of the complex, one for my apartment, one for the mailbox, one for the coffee shop, one for my safety deposit box that has nothing in it, and one for the car I used to drive. I didn't own the car anymore, but I loved that automobile. It was a 1989 Chevy Beretta, and it reminded me of the carefree part of myself that rarely came out.

Anyway, I felt good about the forward progress I made at becoming a more efficient, organized woman of the twenty-first century. I could now look around my box-strewn apartment and know that soon the mess and the things connected to me in some way that I longer wanted would all disappear. I felt uplifted and ready to tackle more of the items on my to-do-list. Melissa would be so proud. Funny how a bunch of carved metal trinkets lining the bottom of my trash can could make a person feel like a million bucks.

I was determined not to lose my gumption, so I headed straight for the closest box marked COLLEGE in bold, Sharpie-black letters. I opened the flaps and sighed. The contents inside propelled me back in time. Images of my dorm days and wild frat parties flittered through my mind. An automatic smile creased my lips.

I missed those days when oodles of homework were my chief concern. When my current grade point average, or how to raise it, was my biggest problem. Oh, how I'd take the stresses of the past—like staying up all night trying to finish a six-page report or cramming for an anatomy test—over the stresses of my present career-world.

I reached in and pulled out a stuffed turtle with the symbols Delta Zeta on its shell. This cute little reptile was the mascot of our sorority, and, for whatever reason, I'd felt the need to purchase him from NKU's campus gift shop my freshmen year. He used to sit on my bed next to the pillow my grandmother embroidered for me. I still had that pillow too, though it was already unpacked and sitting on my bed in the next room.

I clenched my teeth together, finding the strength to say goodbye. A woman in her early thirties had no need for a Greek-alphabetized tortoise. Taking a deep breath, I walked over to the garbage can and tossed him on top of the keys.

Hands on my hips, I stared down at the poor little guy. I couldn't do it.

I grabbed the box with COLLEGE written on the side, dumped it out, and set the empty box next to the garbage can. I scratched out COLLEGE and wrote GOODWILL. I reached into the trash and switched him to his new home. While I was still getting rid of the plush reptile, I felt better that I wasn't sending him to a landfill.

With a nod of affirmation, I went back to the heaping pile of college paraphernalia and decided their fates, one by one. Within an hour, I had sifted through the mementos and had moved onto another box labeled CHILDHOOD.

At this point, I decided to open a bottle of wine. My reasons were two-fold. I had successfully eliminated an entire box from my ownership, and I knew this particular one would take more bravado than I had. From my years of co-existing with hunky jocks and cute frat boys on campus, I came to learn that wine was courage in a bottle.

No sooner had I poured and consumed the first gulp of Pinot Grigio, than I heard a loud noise from the hall. It sounded like someone had tripped and fallen. Concerned, I went to my door and peeked out the security hole. I saw nothing.

I knew I hadn't imagined the sound, and because of how loud it was, my curiosity got the better of me. I unlocked the door and peered out. Lying against the wall, in a contorted fashion, was an unconscious Joseph.

I ran to him and dropped to my knees. "Joseph," I called, giving him a little shake. "Joseph, are you okay?"

He stirred and turned his head in my direction, fanning a wisp of alcohol-infused breath in my face. Whiskey. There was no mistaking that smell. The man had not tripped and knocked himself unconscious...he was drunk. So inebriated he was content to sleep wherever his body had fallen.

"Joseph, you need to get up," I lifted his heavy, dead-weighted arms. He stirred again, but made no effort to help me. Instead, he mumbled a chain of slurred words that made no sense. "Yeah, I know, darlin'," I replied, patronizing him. "You've had a rough night."

"Lonely," he managed to say. "'ts lonely night without you."

I assumed his off-the-cuff admittances were meant for Caroline's ears. I couldn't help but pity him. He was a heartbroken man who'd just lost someone he cared for and had no idea how to deal with it. From the looks of him, getting dumped probably wasn't something he was used to. I imagined he'd done his fair share of breaking hearts in his day, but now that the tables were turned, drinking to forget was the only therapy available to him.

Perhaps if I'd have been more compassionate and appreciative after he'd chased my fruit down the hall, he wouldn't have drank himself into an oblivion. As far as he was concerned, two women had shot him down in the same day. For a man of his caliber, I was sure that was a shocker.

Poor guy.

Although…I had to relish this moment. Even in his drunken stupor, he was beautiful. A hunk of dark, unruly hair had fallen over his brow, and nothing stopped me from brushing it back this time. I took in the strong angles of his face, the way the shadow of scruff across his jaw complimented the high rise of his cheekbones. His lips were full and soft. His nose was straight as an arrow. And he had a small dusting of salt at his temples, making him more appealing to my eyes—as if he wasn't already stunning enough.

I was grateful for this moment. I could admire Joseph fully without anyone knowing. Without *him* knowing. Heck, I could probably strip the man of his clothes and get my eye-full and he'd still be none the wiser given his present condition.

As tempting as that sounded, I worried about how I was going to get him into the safety of his apartment. I couldn't just leave him in the hallway all night. And Lord knows I wasn't going to spend the night chaperoning him as he slept in the hall. I needed my sleep too.

With a deep breath and the sudden determination of ten men, I grabbed his wrists and yanked. "Come on, Joseph. On your feet." I pulled for all I was worth, getting a small response from him.

"Wh'ya doin'?" he slurred as his eyes fluttered opened. "'M try'n to sleep."

"Not out here, you're not," I said, pulling harder. "Come on. Let's get you to your bed."

His head teetered on his shoulders, but he seemed to perk up. "Your bed?" he asked with a crooked smile.

"No, *your* bed," I corrected.

"Th-that's what I said," he stuttered, looking at me like I was an idiot.

I decided to go with it. Anything to get this man on his feet and into his apartment where he belonged, so I could get back to mine. "Yeah, Joseph, I'm taking you to your bed."

He cocked his brow, or tried to. The alcohol in his system had numbed even the muscles in his face. He lugged his heavy arm around my shoulders as if he wasn't the slightest bit intoxicated. He made every effort to be suave, but his speech lacked the smooth debonair quality it required to pull it off. "I though' abou' your bed 'll night. An' how I's gonna make y'call m' name."

Again, I assumed the dirty talk was meant for Caroline and not me. If it wasn't so slurred, the idea might have intrigued me. To a degree, my mind wandered with the notion of what Joseph could do to make me call out his name, but of course, it involved the sober version of him, an adaptation that was too far out of reach.

My mind couldn't dwell in that tantalizing picture for long. He staggered so much, even with me trying to support him, that my brain's focus remained on doing everything in my power to keep him upright.

When we finally faced his door, he leaned forward and rested his head on the wall, his legs beginning to buckle.

"Where are your keys?" I asked, jerking him back to a standing position.

I saw a huge grin slice between his lips. "Ther' in m' pocket."

I knew what he expected. But it wasn't going to happen. "Joseph, reach in your pocket and get your keys."

"You do it," he challenged, his face contorting in a weird expression. I assumed it was his best attempt at arousing me with a not-so smoldering stare.

I rolled my eyes and tried to barter with logic. "Joseph, if I get your keys, I'll have to let go of you, and you'll fall. You've got a free hand...use it."

I heard him sigh before he made a move toward his pocket. I was more thankful than ever when he pulled them out and offered them to me. Unfortunately, his key ring looked like mine, that is, the ring of keys I used to have before I discarded the extras. Struggling to hold him up with my left arm, I sifted through the keys until I found a likely candidate. I used my right hand to attempt to unlock his door. I tried many times to get the damn thing to line up in the slot, but with Joseph's body threatening to collapse at my feet, it wasn't an easy task. On the brink of giving up, I finally got the key to engage and kicked the door open.

The sound jolted his head upward, and his eyes flashed open. "Come in!" he shouted, as if awakened by someone knocking. "Door's open!"

I ignored his drunken outburst and led him into his apartment. Grateful for the large windows that ran the length of the wall in our historical building, I silently thanked God for the blessing of the moonlight pouring in so I didn't have to contend with flipping on a lamp. The evening illumination didn't seem to aid Joseph any, however. In fact, it could have been broad daylight and he still would have stumbled into everything in the room.

Needless to say, I was eager to dump his sorry butt in bed and get back to what I was doing. We wandered aimlessly through his living space, with no guidance from my co-pilot, looking for the bedroom. I did, however, find a guitar leaning against the wall. I smiled. Whether he hammered on the ivories or tickled the frets when composing his songs, I couldn't help but hold him in high regard. Drunk or not, I found this man fascinating.

Moving on, I finally located his bedroom. I ushered him into the spacious room and a waft of cologne tickled my senses as we tottered past his dresser. I couldn't name the cologne, but it certainly smelled wonderful. I imagined him coming out of the shower in his towel and splashing some over his damp neck and shoulders.

What are you doing?

Sorry, I was in a man's bedroom. What did you expect from me?

"Joseph," I said, taking a shot at gaining his attention. When he rolled his head in my direction, he looked at me with the most sincere, pleading eyes. I swallowed, trying to disregard how intense they were when his gaze fell over me. "You're safe in your bedroom now. Just lie down."

"Thanks," he mumbled, and collapsed on the mattress.

I assisted him with hoisting his legs up and removing his shoes and tie. Again, weakling that I am, I thought of taking off his shirt, but I couldn't bring myself to do it. Instead, I pulled the thick duvet over his body and smiled down at him.

One last time, I took this moment to marvel at his raw handsomeness. I doubted I would ever get this chance again. We were on different playing fields, and a guy like him would never be interested in a girl like me.

I touched his face with the back of my fingers and lightly stroked his cheek, never thinking he'd feel it. Evidently, he wasn't as numb as I thought. He opened his eyes and stared at me.

"Jamie," I heard him whisper, though his lips barely moved.

I sat on the edge of the bed and leaned closer so I could hear him. "Yeah?"

"She broke m' heart."

Caroline again. Back to Caroline. That woman didn't deserve as much reflection and consideration as she was getting from this man. I tried my best to comfort him. "I know she did. And I'm sorry you had to go through that."

"S'okay now," he mumbled. "Yer here."

His choice of words threw me. They always say drunk men are honest men, but did my simple presence actually bring Joseph comfort? I contemplated the idea a little longer and eventually came to the conclusion I was putting way too much emphasis on a plastered man's inarticulate remarks. Come morning, he'd have no recollection of this night or what he said to me.

I patted his chest—wow, it was solid—and went back to placating him. "Go to sleep, Joseph. It'll all be better in the morning."

"Stay wit' me…"

I froze. No sooner than I heard his words, I felt his hand rest at the small of my back. Through my T-shirt, I felt the heat of his palm and all five pressure points of his fingertips. His touch ignited feelings I had buried long ago. We locked eyes, and for the span of a few breaths, had I been breathing at all, we both seemed to consider the offer.

No.

I blinked rapidly, affirming I was not going to succumb to something as rash, not to mention reckless and utterly foolhardy, as accepting his proposal. The only reason he asked me to stay was because he was brokenhearted, drunk, and desperate. If he were sober and in his right mind, he would never have made such a suggestion in the first place.

No. I will not be the easy, rebound girl.

"Joseph, you don't know what you're saying. Just close your eyes. You never know…Caroline might come to her senses and call you tomorrow."

"I don' wanna see Caroline 'nymore. She doesn' love me. She doesn' look a' me like you do. I like th' way you look a' me."

Surely, I heard wrong. Perhaps it was my overactive imagination running rampant as I lingered in somewhat of a near embrace with this man. My hand remained on the solid wall of his chest, and his hand still pressed against my back. This position hardly had the makings of a lover's clinch, but considering it had been more than two years since I was this close to a man, I deemed our situation as much of an embrace as one could fathom.

It amazed me that Joseph had thought I looked at him in a manner which evoked significance. I remembered hardly making eye contact with him at all, except for those couple of times I fell entranced by his gaze. Like now.

I looked away and pushed myself from him. He caught my wrist and held me affixed to the side of his bed. The strength in his hand startled me, but the sweet, endearing look in his eyes had me melting.

"Thanks."

With one tiny word, he touched my soul. I opened my mouth to speak, but thank goodness the alcohol had begun to take effect on his attention span before I blurted out something I probably would've regretted.

His eyes fluttered, his head relaxed, and his grip released. His arm dropped and hung off the side of the bed. I reached out and placed it gently across his chest, drawing the covers over him. Within a few seconds, he began snoring.

ABOUT THE AUTHOR

RENEE VINCENT is a *USA Today* bestselling author of romance and women's fiction. Her books have earned numerous accolades, including a #1 Bestseller for Viking Romance.

She lives on a secluded hundred-acre horse farm in the rolling hills of Kentucky with her husband, two beautiful daughters, a couple of nocturnal dogs, and a pair of cats who think they're the masters of the house. Truth be told…they are.

www.ReneeVincent.com

Books By Series

Vikings of Honor Series
Sunset Fire, Book 1
Emerald Glory, Book 2
Souls Reborn, Book 3
Tempered Steel, Book 4

Mavericks of Meeteetse Series
Longing for Langston, Brody & Liv, Book 1
Made for McKinley, Jonas & Ava, Book 2
Falling For Forester, Cole & Crys, Book 3
Wild for Wallace, Sawyer & Charlotte, Book 4

Jamett & Joseph Series
The Start of Something Good, Book 1
The Road to Something Better, Book 2
The Gift of Something Grand, Book 3

Or read books 1 – 3 in one volume:
Something's Bound To Happen

Stand Alone Novel
Silent Partner

Mailing List

Sign up for Renee Vincent's author newsletter and reap the benefits of being one of her loyal subscribers! One lucky winner is drawn each month. What's more, you get a FREE BOOK just for joining.

Go to ReneeVincent.com, then click on "Newsletter" to sign up and start reading!

If you enjoyed this sample book of first chapters by Renee Vincent, please consider leaving an honest review. Reviews not only give credibility to an author's work, they also help other readers find quality books worth reading.

ReneeVincent.com

www.ingramcontent.com/pod-product-compliance
Lightning Source LLC
Chambersburg PA
CBHW030554130626
46552CB00006B/2544